"Shawn Gale's entertaining debut novel...audaciously blends adventure fiction, science-fiction, and fantasy....While the book is aimed at a YA audience, adult readers will find Gale's voice intelligent and insightful and his narrative thematically stimulating.... Contemplative themes of friendship, accountability and redemption notwithstanding, this action-packed adventure featuring a cast of endearing misfits is so addictively page-turning that readers may find themselves finishing the novel in one sitting." ☆ *STARRED REVIEW*
    - *Blueink Review*

"Thoughtful characterization and intriguing world-building come together to make Shawn Gale's *World of Dawn: Arise* an exceptional beginning to what is sure to be a captivating new series....The symbolism woven throughout the narrative is clear and effective.... metaphors and symbolism help bring the nuances of the tale to life. The work ends with several cliffhangers, setting a captivating foundation for the remainder of the series....World of Dawn employs themes of good and evil, courage and cowardice, and guilt and absolution in an appealing novel." ☆☆☆☆
    -*Clarion Review*

Gale's....book is a striking series opener that quickly introduces its titular world while slyly adding engaging elements....A riveting tale and invigorating characters should have readers locked into this adventure series.
    - *Kirkus Review*

Books by Shawn Gale

The Stories That Make Us

World of Dawn Series

Arise
Reveal
The Great Reach
Homeward

WORLD OF DAWN

DAWN

ARISE

SHAWN GALE

To order additional copies of this book, contact:
Xlibris
1-888-795-4274
www.Xlibris.com
Orders@Xlibris.com
722316

The ultimate aim of the quest must be neither release nor ecstasy for oneself, but the wisdom and the power to serve others.
– Joseph Campbell

PROLOGUE

Central Mexico—1914

On Earth there were places more inhospitable than battlefields. San Francisco had become such a place for Ambrose. He was now far away from it, far away from the enticements offered by the civilized world that claimed to have all the answers to modern man's ailments.

The canyon walls rose so high that he thought the sun might shine on the bottom perhaps only a few minutes a day, when at its zenith. Echoing off the walls, the horses' and mule's hooves clipped and clopped, and had been for the last five or so hours during which he and two Mexican cowboys had been following the canyon. It twisted through the countryside, like the diamondback rattler that had struck one of their pack mules day before last, east of Vera Cruz, on a parched flat of cane and acacia stretching for miles.

Turkey vultures drifted in the clear blue sky overhead. They had been ghosting their party for three days. After the mule had succumbed to the rattler's venom, the vultures had been glaringly absent from the sky. That was until this morning when they resumed their lazy, ominous fly-overs. Every once in a while, one crossed the strip of blue overhead, leaving a brief shadow on the canyon floor. Ambrose had come to know the habits of these scavengers intimately when he was a boy in Indiana hunting coyotes with his uncle and father. And he was later reacquainted with them during the Battles of Shiloh and Chickamauga, where they ate the eyes of the dead as if they were appetizers for the feast to come.

He stopped his golden palomino, and the belligerent mule—which was tethered to his saddle—stopped too. The two Mexican cowboys came abreast on their painted quarter horses. Ambrose lifted his tan Stetson and wiped the sweat from his brow with a red handkerchief. He ran a hand through his curly gray hair, then put his hat back on. He reached inside his inner coat pocket and removed a map. It was spotted in rust-colored stains, from the dried blood of its previous owner—a Confederate soldier who had been mortally wounded at the Battle of Kennesaw Mountain in 1864. Ambrose had held the man's shaky, bloody hand—hand of the enemy—in those final moments, while the life poured out of him with every fading pump of his heart. Muttering incoherently, the man reached into his coat and removed the map along with a letter for his young wife back on their plantation in Alabama. Then he handed them both to Ambrose, entrusting him out of desperation. The battle that day had been ferocious; a battle in which Ambrose himself had been severely wounded, when he was shot in the head by a Confederate round, ending his involvement in the war shortly thereafter.

Ambrose unfolded the map and rested it on the horn of his saddle, the canyon draft fluttering the edges. He whispered the words that were on it, written in faded ink, a quatrain he knew by heart: *Up from the Earth's Centre through the Seventh Gate/I rose, and on the throne of Saturn sate/And many a Knot unraveled by the Road/But not the Master-knot of Human Fate.*

"Never have I known this place, señor, and my childhood village is only half a day ride from this ground," said the old cowboy, scratching his salt-and-pepper whiskers. He spit a gob of black chewing tobacco, then twisted in the saddle to look back as if he might have heard something.

"Me neither, señor," said the young cowboy.

Ambrose could tell they were blood relatives as they both had heavy jaws and beady eyes like those of an insect. They were loyal to each other, no doubt about it, a trait he admired no matter how foolish the reasons.

"Because you don't know it, doesn't mean it's never existed," said Ambrose.

The two cowboys looked at each other with a good dose of skepticism. And Ambrose grinned to himself. He was used to this. In San Francisco he had kept the map cloistered away inside the oaken trunk that held his Union Army uniform, service rifle and revolver, and medals and mementos. When he would take the map out to show friends at dinner parties—always after a fair bit of drink—the tattered paper generated much of the same skepticism, usually accompanied by good-humored jeering and laughter. He dealt with it then as he did now: by not paying any attention.

Over the years the map eventually lost its allure as he and his family became more involved in city life, and then as he traveled across the Atlantic to London. Its mystery became relegated to the past like those unforgiving ghosts of war, hidden away but never truly forgotten.

After his marriage crumbled and his two sons died, his life lost all meaning as quickly as a plunge through thin ice. And when writing stories, satire, and criticisms for publication no longer granted their much-needed catharsis, he started to gamble, drink, and carouse.

Then early one morning, after returning from an all-night poker game, he dragged the dusty trunk out from under the bed and flung it open. Feeling the heft of cold steel in his hand instead of the lightness of a pen, he lifted out his Colt revolver for the first time in years and loaded it with a single bullet. He stumbled downstairs and went out into his backyard to where he and his young son had planted Shasta daisies two years before. When he placed the barrel to his temple, the cold steel bit into his skin. He stole his final glance at the sky. And then it surfaced from somewhere deep in his being: The quatrain on the map—word for word—and with this the map's mystery once again intrigued him, compelled him to lower the revolver before the game of Russian roulette had begun—before it had ended.

Over the following few days he wrote letters to family, friends, and colleagues, telling them he was headed to Mexico to report on Pancho Villa's revolt. Then he packed up a few personal belongings and boarded a train for Mexico City. This was how he had come to be there in that canyon.

"One more bend," said Ambrose, folding the map. He slid it into his pocket and nudged his palomino forward, the pack mule following along. No hooves behind him, only whispers in Spanish like a breeze carrying the rumor of uncertain weather. He turned back. The old cowboy jutted his heavy jaw forward and dug heels into the flank of his stallion, sending it into a trot, his nephew following closely behind.

No sooner had the party rounded the bend than their horses neighed loudly and started backing up, spooked. Ahead of them the canyon ended ten horse lengths away. A large opening gaped in the wall like the maw of some hellish fiend none knew existed in this world, but only in the nightmares of small children. Its mouth sucked the air as if drinking life from the world, making strange rasping noises from deep within. The old cowboy shifted awkwardly in his saddle and leaned forward to stare into the darkness.

Ambrose dismounted from his palomino and she stepped back and hoofed the ground. He rubbed her muzzle, whispering soothing words in her ear, but it had little effect on the skittishness she had been exhibiting all morning.

Ambrose left the reins on the saddle horn and went back to the mule. He opened one of the pine supply boxes on its back and took out the naphtha lantern. The mule eyed him anxiously and nudged his hand with its muzzle. Holding the lantern, Ambrose walked past his palomino toward the cave, the draft tugging at his clothes and the hair about his nape. The cowboys remained seated on their horses, silently watching.

Carved in stone above the opening of the cave were worn and faded glyphs that looked as though they were thousands of years old. A stirring aroused in his stomach. The hair on his arms rose. This fascinated him, enticing him forward the way mystery does to those who are brave enough to try to learn of its secrets. As he rested the lantern on a boulder, a black scorpion emerged from the cave's shade and skittered between his legs toward the horses.

He traced his fingertips in the grooves of the glyphs. There were two eyes set directly above the center as though watching for intruders, and below a row of pointed teeth ran the length of the entire top. He turned back to the cowboys. They looked as pale as corpses on display in a funeral parlor.

"I'll scout out the cave," said Ambrose. The old cowboy leaned forward and spat a gob of tobacco. It struck the scorpion, flipping it over. Its legs scurried in the air before it righted itself and skittered off between some rocks.

Ambrose headed into the cave. A moment later his eyes adjusted. The cave sloped down like a gullet leading into the Earth's bowels. This affirmed what he had suspected. He removed a match from his coat pocket and knelt down and struck the match and lit the lantern, catching a whiff of naphtha. Unholstering the Colt revolver on his hip, he thumbed the hammer. During the war enough men had been pounced on by cougars or mountain lions—or even worse, a wounded soldier—upon entering a cave in which they had hoped to find shelter, or a place to hide their spoils.

Without glancing back, he headed farther in. The coolness of the cave enveloped him. His palomino gave a terrified whinny at what she must have thought was her rider being eaten. The cool draft swayed the lantern in his hand, sputtering the flame inside the glass enclosure. He walked down the slope until the opening was no longer visible, only a bit of light from over the brow. There was a hint of dampness in the air. The horses, the cowboys, even the mule were silent as though all were holding their breath, as though waiting to see if some calamity would befall him.

The cave narrowed and the slope steepened downward. He waved the lantern back and forth at a dark that seemed to be living and breathing, almost pulsing against him. Then he saw them on the cave wall: crudely painted ochre images of animals and stick men with spears, like the cave paintings in southern France. He raised the lantern and leaned in close to see a depiction: stick men herding a long line of animals through a circle, like a door or a portal of some type.

A crackling sound suddenly filled the cave. A sound he had not forgotten since the war—a lit dynamite fuse.

He rushed up the slope, lantern swinging wildly in hand. Rifle shots cracked. Rounds struck the ceiling above his head and ricocheted, stone shards stung his face. He dropped the lantern. The flame went out. He ducked another shot that whizzed by his head. Back against the wall, he lifted the Colt and inched slowly up, his heart firing like a cannonade. Then there was a commotion—curses in Spanish, hooves scrambling, the mule braying frightfully. He stepped forward and popped over the brow. He fired three shots at the cowboys' silhouettes. The pack mule charged into the cave, over the spark of the lit dynamite fuse, pine boxes knocking about.

Ambrose whirled around, took four steps down the slope, then leapt. He landed face down and put his arms over the back of his head just in time. The crackle of the fuse silenced for that split second it does before the nitro-glycerine ignited. The explosion shook the cave, buffeting the air, tearing off his Stetson, and pounding his eardrums. Rubble rained down on his body.

The mule scrambled past him, bawling wildly, and cordite-laced dust swirled in the air. He waited for the ceiling to collapse and crush him to death. He cursed himself for not being a better judge of the old cowboy's deceitful character. But why had the scoundrels sealed him in? To rob him of a few meager supplies? Highly unlikely.

He held that position for a minute, allowing the dust to settle. When he felt a nudge against his shoulder, he opened his eyes. His palomino stood over him, eyes wide with fright. He slowly rose from the ground, picked up his Stetson. He coughed and waved at the dusty air. Not a flicker of light remained from the outside world. The exit had been sealed. No matter. He did not plan on using that exit anyhow. No, quite a different exit, or perhaps he should say entrance, an entrance to a far different place.

1

Pacific Northwest—2017

I'd crashed dirt bikes, been bucked off green horses, fallen out of trees, and even rolled an ATV down a hundred-foot embankment once. But when six-foot-three, 220-pound Gregory Parsons ploughed into me as I jumped to make a three-pointer, I figured that I might've learned what it was like to be struck by a speeding truck.

Although I wasn't a 100 percent certain because it happened so fast, it felt like I flipped head over heels before my back thudded on the basketball court's asphalt, blowing the wind from my body and the light from my eyes.

A mighty din roared in my ears as I regained my senses. Blurry, misshapen faces hovered over me, faces that looked like they were reflected in a funhouse mirror. They slowly clarified as the din in my ears faded, their bodies forming. It was Simon and Colby, my two teammates, staring down at me. We were directly under the basketball net, the court's lights shining brightly, hurting the eyes in my throbbing skull.

And for some reason—maybe the intense pain and those lights overhead—I thought of the time I'd broken my right arm during a game of flag football. My seventh-grade teacher, Mr. Campbell, had driven me to the hospital where a doctor plastered my arm in a cast, in a town whose name I'd forgotten, like so many of the others.

Then there was laughter off to my left, lots of it. The spiteful kind, causing my face to warm. I pushed aside the pain. I rolled onto my side, even as Colby and Simon, with voices and hands, told me to lie still. Even though they'd only known me six months, they knew what I wanted to do.

People were shouting from our bleachers, but I couldn't make out what they were saying or maybe at that point I just didn't care. Mr. Conroy strode toward me, the basketball under his arm. Carol's face and hands were pleading for me to stay down. But I figured I'd been down long enough.

The St. Michael's team was standing huddled together, high-fiving and carrying on with laughter. Of course at the center of the revelry was Parsons, a smirk on his face as if proud of his hard foul. He basked in the attention from his team and their supporters. St. Michael's three subs and a flock of girls that I'd seen at previous games stepped onto court. They leaned in close to one another, talking excitedly and giggling, like they'd absolutely enjoyed the hit and were waiting to see what would happen next, as though it was some spectacle.

A firm hand clasped my shoulder and stopped me before I could take another step toward Parsons. Before he turned me around, I knew it was Conroy. He placed his other hand on my other shoulder, leveling his eyes at me, like he did when he was serious and really, really wanted you to listen.

"Enough, cowboy, last thing you need tonight," he said.

Ignoring his words, I tried to jerk free but his hands were clamps. I wanted Parsons as badly as I'd ever wanted anyone before. Though I knew—even heated up as I was—the boys from St. Michael's would try to protect their captain, their leader. Nodding, I bit the inside of my cheek so hard I instantly tasted blood: sweat and coppery. Then, as soon as Conroy let me go, I made my move.

I turned and dashed toward Parsons, who was too busy boasting, unaware that I was headed straight for him. I closed the distance with the speed of a starving mountain lion zeroing in on its first meal in days. By the time the St. Michael's boys spotted me, they didn't have enough time to prepare a defensive position. I leapt, thudding into shoulders and stirring cries, and collided with Parsons.

We both went down hard, cursing and clutching at each other. People were shouting. Then body after body dog-piled me, and with each successive one, more weight added until I was gasping for air, feeling intense pressure building on my upper torso. It felt like my sternum was about to crack wide open and splay out like week-old roadkill. Tiny flashes danced in my vision, and for the second time within a minute, my world went black, very black.

When I came around this time, no one was on top of me, no distorted teammates' faces hovering, or basketball net high above. I was spread-eagle on my back, on my own. The first thing I heard was my heart reverberating loudly in my skull, and then a voice off to the right, Mr. Bobbitt's, the St. Michael's coach: "*Every* single time your boys play, something like this happens, Conroy—every time! To the point where I might need to hire security for our *friendly* three-on-threes. All because your boys can't control themselves."

"*Friendly*? You'd have to bury your head in the sand to miss the fouls your players make," said Conroy, gesturing his free hand like he did when he was all worked up, "and Parsons tried to cut him in half."

"It's called the competitive edge," said Mr. Bobbitt, hands on his hips, face-to-face with Conroy.

The boys from St. Michael's were walking toward their bleachers. A large group of twenty-five or so supporters had begun to step down to praise their win. The score had been 45-45, with only a few seconds remaining when I'd taken my jump shot. A basket would've secured the win for Halton House, making it our second win in the eleven games we'd played against St. Michael's over the previous four months.

I pushed my aching body to my feet and began to slowly limp toward our bleachers, where Colby and Simon were sitting beside Conroy's two nieces, Anna and Tabby. The St. Michael's janitor, Mr. Wilkes, stood at the end of our bleachers, leaning on a wooden push broom next to a steel garbage can. Whenever we played, Mr. Wilkes watched from the sidelines near our bleachers, puttering around like a non-entity. No one seemed to notice him there, except for me, and definitely not his school's team.

As I limped, I heard Conroy and Mr. Bobbitt still going at each other. "Anything like this happens again," said Mr. Bobbitt. "I'll inform the City Council—your crew of *misfits* will be done this year instead of next year."

Misfits? That was new. Troubled youth, wayward youth, juvenile delinquents, troublemakers, even hellions once, but I'd never heard us boys at Halton House referred to as "misfits." And what did he mean by finished this year instead of next year?

"Educate your team on sportsmanship. You know—that thing called coaching," said Conroy, chest-passing the basketball to Mr. Bobbitt, with just a little too much force.

I sat on the bench. Mr. Bobbitt scowled and shook his head like he always did, as if disgusted. Then he spun around and marched toward the St. Michael's bleachers. Parsons trotted out to meet him halfway. The two spoke in hushed voices. Parsons glared at me, flipped me the bird. Even from a distance, I could hear them chuckling. This was a Catholic team, from a Catholic school?

When Parsons and Mr. Bobbitt arrived at their bleachers, players and supporters thronged them, patting them on the back like they'd saved a family from a burning house, or beat a pack of "misfits" in a basketball game.

Our bleachers, on the other hand, were as somber and silent as a graveyard at midnight. Colby and Simon's heads were lowered, looking down into their gym bags, defeated, and totally demoralized. Once again.

"You gonna live?" said Conroy, suddenly beside me.

"Yeah, guess it was pretty stupid going after him like that," I said.

Conroy was quiet for a moment. "Come on," he said, "let's get out of here before both of us get piled on."

St. Michael's bleachers emptied as they headed out to their vehicles in the parking lot, still celebrating their victory.

"I take it you didn't hear me warning you about Parsons?" said Conroy.

"Nah, just heard screams," I said, leaning forward to untie my Reeboks.

"For Catholics they're awfully angry," said Mr. Wilkes, removing a bag from a garbage can. "Make you think it was UFC, not basketball."

"Romans did build coliseums for gladiators," said Simon.

"Where'd that come from?" said Colby.

"You know, Roman Catholics—gladiators—UFC."

"Roman Catholics didn't build coliseums," said Anna. "Roman *emperors* first built what were called amphitheaters before Catholicism—at the time they worshiped gods like Apollo, Mercury, and Neptune—then they went on to build coliseums."

"What are you talking about?" said Simon.

"One of her egghead comments she always making," said Colby. "Always correcting everything—how you know all this shit anyhow?"

Anna shrugged, not bothering to answer him.

I swiped the imbedded gravel from my knee and shin, arousing a sting. A scrape ran the length of my lower leg—red, raw, and deep—and I wondered if I'd have another scar to add to the dozens of others on my body. The scars that caused one of my mother's friends to say she was glad I didn't belong to her.

Colby sucked his teeth, and said, "Told you it was stupid to go after pretty-boy Parsons."

"Thanks for watching out," I said, kicking off my shoes. "Nice of you both to have my back. Way to be teammates."

"You knew Parsons was gunning for you, jughead," said Colby, pouring some bottled water onto his gym towel, to wipe clean his prized Nike Airmaxes.

"No way they'd let us win again," said Simon. "Remember how devastated they were last time we kicked their ass? So much steam came out of Bobbitt's head, I thought he was going to blast off to the space station."

"Bobbitt's a meatball," said Colby. He and Simon fist-bumped

Tabby tittered, and said, "A giant meatball." Conroy gave her a disapproving look.

I tugged off my knee brace. "And so what? I'm supposed to sprout a big all-seeing eyeball in the back of my head? That's what my teammates are for. Watch my back. Make sure jerks don't wallop me."

"Okay, guys, let's simmer down," said Conroy. He stood in front of us. "We'll get them next time."

Colby stuffed his towel into his gym bag. "You say that same crap every time. And we never get them next time. We lose, lose, lose. We gonna lose next time too—team of losers." He sucked his teeth again, and I was sure if his skin wasn't so black, he'd be flushed red. He picked up his gym bag and stormed off toward the parking lot.

Conroy began to say something to Colby, when Carol stepped off the bleachers. "I'll talk to him. Meet you guys at the van," she said in her motherly tone.

I tossed my knee brace into my gym bag and watched them leave. She'd been babying him more than usual over the last few weeks. Family problems back in Detroit, something to do with an aunt whose boyfriend sold a bunch of her things to pay a gambling debt, real inner-city-drama-type stuff.

"He's pouting like he's the one who got creamed and almost crushed to death," said Simon.

"He's always a grump," said Anna. She stepped down from the bleachers, her gym-bag-sized maroon Gucci purse slung over her shoulder. As always, she worked her iPhone, texting or surfing or playing a brain game or whatever else she did. It baffled me how she could remain so focused on that little screen while at the same time walk, talk, and shop. Sometimes all three at once without lifting her eyes.

"Grump. More like a grouch," said Tabby.

"Hey, enough, guys," said Conroy. "Let's grab our gear and hit the road."

"You think Hena's going to give birth to her colt tonight?" said Tabby.

"Might've happened already. Barley Charlie'll take care of her," I said, and I stood up with my gym bag.

"We'll call Charlie on the drive home," said Conroy, "find out how he's making out."

Simon had put on his Skull Candy headphones already. He began walking beside me, gym bag dangling by his knee. Across the courts in the far parking lot, where St. Michael's parked, a silver BMW SUV was the last vehicle leaving.

"Why do you think they park so far away from us all the time?" said Simon, fixed on the BMW's rear end.

"Maybe they don't want us contaminating their vehicles," I said.

"They probably think you'll steal them," said Anna.

"And you know this because?" I said.

"Because those are *her* type of people—rich and stuck-up," said Simon jokingly.

"Okay, okay," said Conroy. "Let's go." He zipped up his green army duffel bag and put his arm around Tabby's shoulder and followed us. We drifted toward the parking lot. As we left, Mr. Wilkes was picking up garbage under the St. Michael's bleachers with a garbage picker. I gave a wave as we passed through the gate, unsure if he'd seen me at first until he looked up and waved back.

"Don't be so hard on yourself. You don't need to prove yourself to anyone," said Conroy. "Besides, the past is where we've been—"

"And the future is where we're going," I said, finishing the saying. Conroy loved his quotes, sayings, and proverbs. He owned books and books of them from which I'd learned dozens since arriving at Halton House.

"You're getting good with those," he said proudly.

"Maybe not good enough."

2

After we were all seated in our usual spots in Halton House's white Chevy van—Conroy driving, Carol riding shotgun, Tabby and Anna on the middle bench, and us three boys sitting in the back—Conroy started the engine. Carol reminded everyone to buckle up, as she always did. If Conroy filled the role of father at Halton House, Carol filled that of mother. Sometimes she was over the top, harping on us to floss every night, giving us tips on how to brush our teeth, wash our hands for the duration of "Twinkle, Twinkle Little Star," wash our bedding at least twice a week, stuff like that.

Conroy wheeled out of the parking lot onto Threshold Drive. It was canopied by hardy oaks and lined by cozy-looking houses with cedar fences, garden gnomes, Bambis, and other lawn ornaments. It was the epitome of family, of stability. Things us three boys hadn't had much of prior to arriving at Halton House.

Two minutes later, we turned onto Highway 10, classic rock playing on the radio. I picked up *All the Pretty Horses,* which I tried to read in the dim orange glow filtering in from the streetlights. Simon hadn't removed his headphones. His head bobbed slightly to whatever dance music that he was listening to. Colby stared out the window at passing vehicles.

"Gross," huffed Tabby. "All I can smell is your moldy army bag, Uncle Brad, and *their* B.O." She unlatched and opened the small side window. Whistling air filled the interior.

"Bet you wouldn't say that if we won the game," said Colby quietly.

"And that would have made you smell like . . . roses?" said Tabby.

"Ah, post-game odor," said Conroy. "You're telling me you never dealt with funny smells during your swim meets?"

"Funny, not funky. Mostly chlorine," she said.

"I'll take B.O. over chlorine any day," I said.

Colby sucked his teeth. "Man, I should be driving one of those Corvettes right now or maybe that Suburban right there, that black one."

"We can start studying for your license next week," said Carol cheerfully.

Colby gave a little laugh, and said, "Never needed one before."

"And why are you here again?" I said.

"He's a klepto," said Anna, eyes glued to her iPhone. "Can't go without stealing."

"Getting caught up with some white-boy backstabbers is all," said Colby. He turned to Anna. "And look who's talking. High-society princess. No crown or prince, shoveling shit at the farm, mucking out chicken coups."

"Kiss off," she said. "You don't know anything about me . . . you . . . thug! You and your fake gold chain."

Colby lifted his hands like he was trying to ward off bad juju. "Oh, oh, big bad thug gonna huff and puff and blow your house down," he said, half-laughing. "And my chain ain't fake, like your fake-ass ring."

Anna lifted her finger, which happened to be her middle. "This is an 18k gold puzzle ring given to me by my grandmother—FYI."

Colby turned away, not bothering to look. "At least I ain't listening to that crappy '80s retro you always playing on your phone. And who got Duran Duran for a ringtone anyway?"

"Oh, let me guess, if it's not singing about hoes, bling, and popo on the block, you're not down with it. Is that it? You're such a cliché. And it's INXS—the ringtone."

"Okay, guys. Cool it," said Conroy. "We've had long day—up early, chores, long drive, big game."

"You mean big defeat," I said.

"Oh, even Mr. Happy's got a losing attitude now," said Colby.

"Better than a bad attitude," said Tabby.

"I said cool it, guys," said Conroy, his voice uncharacteristically high.

I went back to *All the Pretty Horses*, not because I really expected to read any of it, but because I didn't want to be involved in the conversation any longer. It was the type that always seemed to have someone on the losing end. The dull thump from Simon's headphones increased in volume, like he'd turned it up to drown out the conversation. I guess we all had our own way to deal with things.

Right before I asked Carol to turn up the Rolling Stones' tune on the radio—"Paint It Black"—she turned the volume down and asked us if we'd like to call Charlie, find out Hena's status.

Everyone in the back gave a unanimous *yes*, except for Simon who was leaning back, eyes shut, as if he was drifting along to his music and couldn't be bothered by anything.

With Hena on the verge of giving birth, we'd all discussed canceling the game that morning. But Conroy said Mr. Bobbitt would most likely lodge a complaint with City Council. Although Conroy didn't say it, that would give more ammo for Mr. Bobbitt to use against Halton House, exactly what he wanted. We all knew that almost half of City Council had voted against allowing Mr. Conroy to open Halton House, citing all sorts of wild examples of issues that could possibly arise: a gambling den, a marijuana grow-op, and the craziest one—we might start capturing and ritually sacrificing neighborhood pets, like some kind of cult.

Carol twisted back in her seat, facing her cellphone toward us, which started to ring on speakerphone.

Ahead on the highway, something was going on. Yellow and orange lights flashed brightly.

"Everyone buckled up?" said Carol, still holding her ringing phone.

"*Yes*," everyone groaned tiredly. We jostled around in the back of the van to get a clearer view of what was taking place up ahead, like a bunch of excitement junkies. Conroy slowed down as we approached the lighted road barriers and other smaller white road signs that barred the highway.

"Looks like a crime scene," said Colby. "Maybe an accident, lots of twisted steel—don't see any ambulances though."

"You'd like that, wouldn't you?" said Anna, scoffing.

"It's municipality workers," said Conroy.

A white municipality truck was parked in front of the signs, its hazard lights on. In the center of the highway stood a road worker wearing a white hardhat and an orange reflective safety vest. As we approached, he lifted a yellow road sign with the word STOP in large black letters. There was no oncoming traffic. A line of a dozen or so vehicles had formed behind us, with more adding to it every moment.

"Must be serious," said Tabby.

Charlie's voicemail picked up, and Carol held her cellphone near her mouth and said she wasn't sure when we'd be home because the highway north of the city was shut down. She asked him to call us back when he got the message.

"Definitely an accident, main highway shut down like this," said Colby.

"You and your morbid infatuations," said Anna.

"Who's talking to you?" he fired back.

"Let's find out what's happened," intervened Conroy.

We stopped before the road worker and barrier. Conroy put the van in park and lowered the window, night air instantly cooling the inside of the van. The orange lights made a whirling sound. Somewhere in the distance heavy machinery hummed and hydraulics whined and steel knocked and scrapped against rock. I made out some machines ahead on the highway, moving around, their lights flashing.

Everyone in the van went quiet, repositioning to get a better look. Carol shut the radio off as the heavyset road worker neared Conroy's window. His hardhat was scuffed and plastered in stickers, like he'd been wearing it for years. The sign dangled by his thigh, and he carried a smoke in his other hand. He took a drag and tossed the butt before coming to the window.

Tabby scoffed, and said, "What a scuzzball." She'd made her dislike for smokers and litterers well-known. Especially the latter after Colby had carelessly thrown out a Subway wrapper from the van's window as we were on our way to a local farmers' market a few days back.

"Sir, gonna have to ask you to turn around. The highway's closed. Landslide hit about two hours ago," said the road worker.

"What's the time frame for it to be cleared?" said Conroy.

The road worker looked toward the machines, tilting his head back and forth, as if he was trying to get an idea.

"Uh, open tomorrow morning at the earliest. We'll be here all night cleaning up."

Sighs went through the van, bodies thudded back into their seats.

"Was anyone hurt?" said Carol.

"No, ma'am, but it lifted a house clean off its foundation though, carried it for a half a mile. Family wasn't home, on vacation in Mexico, thankfully."

"Must have been a good size," said Conroy.

"Yup, usually are this time of year. A bad spring for landslides. More on record than ever. Two others in the last forty-eight hours," he said, and looked back toward the city. There was a long line of vehicles behind us now. I figured he'd probably repeat what he'd just said a thousand more times tonight, like a voice recording on one of those automated services.

"If you're heading north tonight, gonna need to take Highway 7 . . . or stay in town till morning. Our supervisor will be calling the local radio station every hour to give an update."

"Thanks, you have a nice night and be safe," said Conroy.

"I think Mother Nature's done for the night," he said.

Carol bobbed down in between the seats. "Oh, would you like a bottle of water? We have some in the cooler."

"No thanks, ma'am, got my thermos in the truck. Sorry for the inconvenience. Hopefully you can make it to your destination," he said, and stepped back and waved the sign for us to turn around.

Conroy wound the window up. He wheeled the van around on the highway and headed south, the lights from the city a glowing dome on the horizon. We passed the long line of vehicles, which already had to be a mile in length. Yup, the road worker would have to repeat himself *at least* a thousand more times tonight.

"Be a lot of peeved-off motorists," said Conroy. "Okay, so, we got three options, guys. We take Highway 7, looking at three hours.

Stay at a hotel in the city, nothing fancy. Or, take Windigo Road up around the backside of Mount Romni, make it home in an hour."

Carol's cellphone rang and she answered.

"I'm saying hotel," said Colby. "No way am I sitting for three hours. And last time we drove Windigo Road, my fillings rattled out of my head."

"You're right. It is a rough ride, especially this time of year," said Conroy. "Doubt they've been up there filling in spring potholes yet."

"He's right about the three hours," said Anna. "It's too long, especially with this company."

"I third that," said Tabby.

"I fourth that," I said. "Three hours is too long."

"Charlie's on speakerphone," said Carol, turning back, holding up her cellphone. "He's got news."

"Hello," said Charlie. "Can everyone hear me?"

"*Yes*," said everyone.

"Looks like Hena and her colt aren't waiting any longer. Her water broke a half hour ago. She's in labor."

"We have a little problem, Charlie," said Conroy. "Highway's been shut down about ten miles north of the city. There's been a landslide. Doesn't look as though it'll be clear until morning at the earliest. We haven't decided whether or not we're staying in the city or taking Windigo Road. How are you managing?"

"Hunky dory. Not my first rodeo. My son's coming over to help anyhow. Be here any minute now."

That was typical Charlie, always upbeat, always okay, a good ol' boy that could be in the midst of the apocalypse, and would somehow find a way to be *hunky dory.*

"This sucks. We've been waiting forever, now we're gonna miss it," said Tabby.

"Okay, Charlie, can you keep your phone on and we'll call back as soon as we figure this out?" said Conroy.

"Roger that," said Charlie, and then hung up.

"Well, looks like we got two options then," said Conroy. "Let's see a show of hands."

"Always voting for everything," said Colby. "Just make the call—you know everyone wants to go home tonight. So just take the bone rattler." Colby wasn't big on the whole voting thing, thought it childish, and griped every single time.

"All right," said Carol, "all in favor of staying in a hotel."

Colby and Anna raised their hands. How ironic. The two personalities that clashed the most at Halton House were now voting together. Colby backhanded Simon's shoulder. Simon slid his headphones down to his neck. "You want to stay in the city or take Windigo Road home?" said Colby.

"Windigo Road," said Simon without a second hesitation.

"All in favor of Windigo Road?" said Carol.

Simon, Tabby, and I raised our hands. Team Windigo.

Colby sucked his teeth and shaking his head, looked out the window.

"And Windigo Road it is," said Carol. "A healthy micro-democracy."

"Those three always vote together," said Colby. "Always the same."

"Guess you're on the wrong team," I said.

"Guess you three suck," said Colby.

Simon slid his headphones back on.

"I'm sick and tired of your big mouth," I said. "Like a broken record playing the same annoying song, over and over and—"

"That's enough," said Conroy. "We'll get home tonight, all get to see Hena's colt. Maybe even come up with a name."

"Gonna be another vote for that too?" said Colby sarcastically.

"You're such a baby," said Tabby.

It became silent then. Anna passed her iPhone to Tabby to show her something on the screen. Carol and Conroy talked quietly to each other. Everyone settled into their usual driving routines, in their own little worlds inside the little van, close to one another yet still so far apart. I took it all in for a minute, wondering if I was the only one who paid any attention to it, saw it the way I did. Maybe I was the only one who cared enough to ask those kinds of questions. I don't know. Everyone else seemed content only when closed off from one another. Don't get me wrong. There were fleeting moments of unity, when we all worked together to complete a task, not on the basketball court so much but when we fed the chickens or the heifers or calves or bulls, or fixed sections of fence or even mucked out the barns. During those times, everyone seemed to enjoy one another's company.

"How about we stop and pick up some snacks at the Shell," said Carol.

A unanimous *yes* went through the back of the van. Even from Simon who was wearing his headphones. It was nice to see that we all came to common ground, on at least one thing.

3

The Shell station could be seen from miles away, bright against Mount Romni's blackness. The upper half of the exterior walls were glass, making visible the shelves and fridges stocked with their usual gas station fare. We'd stopped there at the tail end of last winter when we'd driven to the city to play against St. Michael's—our second or third game—and driven by it a few other times.

Conroy pulled up to the pump. The parking lot was empty. Our van was the only vehicle, which made me wonder how the clerk got to work until I noticed a high-end mountain bike locked up at the bike rack. I couldn't recall ever seeing the station completely empty, like it was. Carol, Tabby, and Colby climbed out as soon as Conroy shut the engine off. They all made a beeline for the entrance.

"You guys aren't going in?" said Conroy, looking back at us. "Snacks are on Carol."

"The majority of what they sell is high-glycemic carbs anyway—I got something here," said Anna. She dug in her purse for one of those fruit-and-nut bars she packed around, the ones she could only buy at the health food store. Whatever she ate or drank needed to pass a rigorous food analysis in which she scrutinized food labels. Simon hadn't removed his headphones, and didn't seem interested whatsoever in moving. I stuffed *All the Pretty Horses* into the seat's back pouch and exchanged it for my plastic camouflage change purse.

"My legs are stiff as boards," I said, and maneuvered around the middle-bench seat. I climbed out of the side sliding door that Colby hadn't shut all the way.

Lifting my arms above my head, I leaned backward, then bent over and touched my toes a few times. I tilted my head back against a cool breeze sweeping down from Mount Romni, carrying a wild, raw earthy scent. For a moment, I was reminded of standing on the deck of the *Coho* ferry a few months before, when Conroy and Carol had taken us all over to visit Victoria on Vancouver Island. It'd been my first trip to Canada.

Stars shone dazzlingly, the honey-colored moon almost full. As the gas pump hummed, I cut across the parking lot toward the lit vending machine from which I'd bought a Gatorade last time we stopped for gas. Anna watched me through the van window. The others glided around the aisles in the Shell, their heads seemingly hovering above the shelves.

I dug out a dollar twenty-five, dropped it into the slot, and pressed the button for Orange Gatorade. A bottle clunked down the chute. When I stooped to pick it up, someone cleared their throat. I glanced around, thinking one of the others had come up behind me. No one was there, only Conroy back at the van still pumping gas, Simon and Anna's silhouettes visible through the tinted windows. Then I heard it again, only louder this time.

I peeked around the far side of the vending machine. An old Indian man was sitting in a plastic patio chair, back to the wall. A black cowboy hat, faded and dusty, rested on his head with a large eagle feather tucked in a band around the brim. Tiny black eyes stared at me from his wrinkly, dusky face.

"Beer," he said, and tapped the machine with a crooked finger.

I waited a moment for him to say more, but he didn't. That was it. One word—beer.

"There's no beer in here, mister," I said, scanning the labels, trying not to chuckle.

He pointed again, and said, "Beer," more loudly.

Again I scanned the labels, and again I came up empty. I thought that he might've been suffering from one of those diseases that old people get, like Alzheimer's or dementia, or maybe he was just clogged up with cobwebs. Then I saw it: the very last label at the bottom was Root Beer. Smiling to myself, feeling kinda stupid for not getting it the first time, I quickly dumped the rest of the change into my palm and dropped a dollar worth of quarters into the slot. "You want a beer, I'll get you one." I hit the button. The can clunked down the chute. When I handed it to him, he gave me the widest smile, revealing a perfect set of white teeth that would've given Anna's pearls a run for their money.

An electronic bell dinged from the Shell's entrance, and I heard the others' voices as they cut across the parking lot toward the van. Conroy met Carol halfway and they walked to the van together, laughing at something one of them had said. If I didn't know them, I'd have thought them a couple. Looking back, who knows? Maybe they were. Maybe they were and they'd kept it hidden from all of us.

The old Indian cleared his throat again, then opened his hand, palm up. Inside rested a small leather pouch on a thong. I waved him off. "You don't need to trade, old-timer. Got plenty of change at home. Consider it a gift."

He thrust his hand forward and nodded, urging me to take it, as if he wasn't prepared to take *no* for an answer. I figured he didn't speak English that well, or maybe not at all, otherwise he would've said some more words to get his message across. Then I thought maybe he was partially mute. But what was the big deal? The old Indian wanted to trade, so might as well let him, right? I plucked the pouch from his hand and held it up for a look. It was nothing fancy: a worn piece of brown leather sewn into a teardrop shape, with a strip so you could hang it around your neck. There was something inside. I dumped out a stone into my hand. Tiny, smooth, shiny, and black. Could've switched it for one of his eyes and you wouldn't ever know the difference. He gave a wheezy chuckle and nodded vigorously, like I'd done something he thought mighty right.

Two quick honks blared from the van, signaling it was time for me to scoot. I put the stone back inside and hung the pouch around my neck, under my shirt.

"Thanks, old-timer," I said. "I'll keep it forever, pass it on to my kids."

He nodded again, this time gently. He touched his temple, heart, and then his temple again. He spoke in a language that reminded me of Cherokee, like he was praying or singing a few lyrics from a song. I'd been around Cherokee ranch hands at Vince's ranch in Montana, Whispering Cedars, the last place my mother and I'd lived together before life got all messed up. I'd heard those Cherokee speak their musical language when no one else was around, as if it was taboo for them to speak it around anyone but their own people. As the last word left his lips, the horn blared again.

"I got to get a move on, mister. You take care of yourself. Thanks for the pouch and stone. I hope that beer wets your whistle."

He smiled to reveal those teeth again, and gave a little wave of his hand, all the while his eyes sparkling. I left him rocking back and forth—cowboy boots crossed in front of him, bouncing to a rhythm only he could hear—and I trotted back to the van. The others had already started eating their snacks by the time I took a seat beside Anna, who was on her iPhone again. Nothing new there. I was starting to think it was her auxiliary brain.

Carol reminded everyone—of course—to buckle up. As Conroy pulled out of the Shell, I turned to where the old Indian had been sitting, but the lawn chair was empty and he was nowhere in sight. I figured he moved quicker than he looked.

4

Conroy drove north on the rural road that ran along the base of Mount Romni, whose mass obscured the honey moon and a good deal of the sky. I'd once heard that if you saw the honey moon, it meant a bountiful harvest, and I found myself wondering if that meant bountiful hay in the Pacific Northwest too, hay Halton House would start baling in a few months.

There still wasn't enough light, so I didn't bother to try to read again. Instead, I just sipped my Gatorade as we passed the farms off to the left. Simon used his book light to read a *Popular Science,* as everyone else did their usual thing.

When we neared Windigo Road, Conroy slowed down and flicked his blinker on, and Carol—once again—reminded everyone to make sure they were buckled up.

And again, there was a drone of *yeses.*

"Ya'll ready for the bone rattler?" said Colby. "Coming up."

"It's not that bad," I said.

"Guess if you're riding horses since you were in diapers like you it ain't. But in Detroit we riding strictly Cadillacs," he said, making a waving motion with his hand.

"You said you were busted in Boise for stealing ride-on lawnmowers," said Simon. "Does Cadillac make ride-on lawnmowers now?"

Everyone in the rear of the van began to laugh. Colby tried to speak up but only managed a stammer. The laughter died down, and Colby said, "That was one time. One lawnmower, and it was on a trailer behind a Ford King Ranch. Shit, look who's flapping. Who burns up logging trucks? Stupidest thing I ever heard anybody do. You ain't even make money doing that."

"Hey, what did we agree on, guys?" said Conroy.

"Yeah, yeah, I know," said Colby, turning back to the window. "We been at it for five months."

"Actually six months," said Anna, looking up from her iPhone. "Because Tabby and I arrived one month ago and you'd all been at Halton House for five months prior."

"Always got be a know-it-all," said Colby. "Always got to be right 'bout everything."

"I'm just saying," said Anna, going back to what she was doing.

Carol turned around. "It's not that we don't trust you guys. But it's important to look at those past actions in a safe environment and understand they were actions that you did, and not who you are."

"And I thought we agreed—no sermonizing in the van," I said.

Even in the dimness, Carol's blush was visible, reminding me she was only in her late twenties, fresh out of some prestigious university in Wisconsin.

"And what about you?" said Tabby, turning to me. "Colby the car thief, Simon the eco-terrorist. Why is Tanner Kurtz here?"

I took a long drink from my Gatorade, pretending not to hear the question, hoping she wouldn't ask again.

"Oh, buckaroo don't like to talk 'bout all the banks he robbed," said Colby. "They call his uncle and him Butch Cassidy and the Sundance Kid. Couple Wild West bank robbers."

Sure, I'd heard what the news had been calling us. But I didn't like it one bit.

"Wait, that was you?" said Anna. "Oh, oh, that's too funny."

"Yeah, why don't you tell 'em, stop acting like you're better than us," said Colby.

"I never said I was better than anyone."

"Never said it but you acting like it all the time," said Colby.

"Says who?"

"Says me, that's who."

"You are *gonzo* sometimes, man," I said, shaking my head. "What world do you live in?"

He got in my face. "What world? What world do I live in?"

"Yeah, that's what said," I shot back, my fists balling.

"That's enough," said Conroy, his voice loud and firm.

We all knew that we were only supposed to talk about our crimes during the once-a-week one-on-one sessions, or during the group sessions that we participated in one hour daily, five days a week, in the living room at Halton House. Those were safe places, where criticizing didn't happen. We shared about our lives, what happened leading up to our crimes, the crimes themselves, and the consequences afterwards—arrest, incarceration, court, and sentencing. They were places we shared about the harm our crimes caused ourselves and others. All the ugly stuff. All the things that led us to Halton House, a farm created to give youth a second chance to better themselves instead of a jail sentence at a youth detention facility. Simon, Colby, and I were all from different walks of life. Simon was from a Snohomish Indian reserve near Seattle. He'd got caught up with his mother's boyfriend and his crew of eco-terrorists. Colby was from Detroit. He'd moved to Boise, Idaho, and started boosting cars and trucks and selling them to a local chop shop. And me, well, I'd spent my childhood in the Midwest and then lived in eight states in four years before my mother died. Then I went on to knock off twelve banks with my uncle Hanker in Colorado, Montana, and Washington, an act of notoriety that seemed to define my every waking moment for the last eight months.

Although our stories were different, they all had one common thread: We were headed for a life in and out of prison, if we didn't clean up our acts. During a group session, I shared the story of the night I was arrested. How I heard motors revving outside the room of the highway motel Uncle Hanker and I had been holed up in. I'd peeked through those heavy curtains to see black SUVs, then tact team members rushed out wearing black helmets and suits, like modern-day armor, carrying automatic rifles. I'd told them how they battered the door off the hinges and charged in, poised to shoot if we showed any signs of resistance. That'd been the most frightening event of my young life, scary as I imagined hell was, preparing for those bullets to rip into my body, to end me, kaput, dead, finished, joining my mother wherever she was, if anywhere. And maybe joining my father as well, if he was dead and not just in some other state or country, living with a new family, raising a new son. I'd relived that motel event more times than I could count, had more nightmares about it than I thought possible. The mornings after, I'd always be left wondering if the bank employees and customers at those banks we'd robbed had been having them too.

5

Conroy turned onto Windigo Road. The van bounced over potholes. Music played quietly on the radio—some Top 40 song I thought I recognized but couldn't name for certain. We continued to ascend, and soon the road veered farther into the mountainside, firs and cedars rising up to block the farm road and low-lying land. The road got rougher the higher we went, and when the van started to buck like a bronco, Conroy slowed down to try and navigate around the deeper holes.

"Hey, you guys hear that?" said Tabby, looking out the window toward the mountain.

"That's Simon's music," said Colby. "Always thumping the fruity dance music."

"It's off," said Simon. His headphones were still on. "She's right, I hear it too."

Right then and there, I figured he probably did that all the time. Pretending to listen to his iPod when in fact he was slyly listening to what was going on around him.

Anna pressed her face against the window, her breath causing condensation. "Sounds like a plane flying overhead." She drew a heart, and then smeared it.

I rested my palm on a section of the plastic panel. "Planes don't shake the ground," I said, feeling a vibration. "It feels like a train."

Someone turned the volume down on the radio, and Carol turned toward the mountain, then screeched like a banshee.

An undulating mass of darkness surged toward us.

Screams, wails, and shrieks enveloped the van, so terrifyingly loud that my eardrums felt like they might burst. The mass struck the van with the force of a train. Windows imploded, metal buckled and sheared. Earth flooded into the blown-out windows. A blast of it hit my face, filling my mouth and nostrils. A tree trunk rammed the front end and spun the van three-sixty. Then a tree branch impaled the passenger side window, inches away from my face, and speared right on through the other side, showering us with glass shards. Next the van flipped onto its side, contents flying about, bodies slamming and thudding against one another. The screaming intensified, as if it was from wild animals being slaughtered, and the landslide carried us swifter and swifter until it swept us over an edge that I couldn't see but only feel. The van rolled onto its roof, glass shards cutting my face and arms. I was upside down, the seatbelt violently jerking into my waist. My guts beat my insides like a bowling ball.

The screams, rumbling earth, and shearing metal and snapping branches merged into a horrifying sound that I didn't know could exist. My body tensed, preparing for the van to peel open, for the darkness to engulf us. I knew we were all about to die. Then the van flipped onto its side, then back onto its roof. It rotated once, then twice, and then a third time, like a spinning top that picked up speed with each revolution—again and again and again. I choked on the earth in my mouth, then all went dark.

6

An electronic pinging noise roused me from the darkness. I tasted grit. I tasted the coppery tang of blood in my mouth, the air thick with gasoline vapor. Trying futilely to piece together what had happened, I wiped my hand across my raw eyes and began to frantically pat my body to ensure I hadn't broken anything, wasn't missing a limb, or bleeding out and just didn't know it yet.

The van's interior was crumpled, and it took a moment for me to get my bearings and realize the van now lay on its passenger side. A limp body slumped against me—unconscious or maybe even dead. At that point I had no idea. Suddenly a sharp pain shot through my hip, from the seatbelt digging into my hip bone. I braced my arm against the plastic interior, unbuckled myself, and dropped against the paneling with a thud.

Standing up on unfirm footing, I strained my eyes, making out shapes—seats, bodies, the remains of windows like tattered spider webs, and mud, rock, tree branches, and other plant debris.

A landslide had struck the van on Windigo Road. That much I knew. And now we were buried somewhere in it. Questions flooded me: How deep were we? How far had we been carried? A half a mile like that house? A mile or maybe two? Was anyone else still alive? Would I die? Would we all die? I was shocked by the extent to which the van had been crushed. I thought of a stomped popcan. Simon's body dangled lifelessly against me like a broken doll.

"Simon, Simon," I said, tugging his arm. My heart was racing.

No words, no movement, nothing at all. I couldn't tell whether he was alive or dead. Colby was on the other side of him, slumped against a mound of earth that'd thrust into the van. One of the girls was there amidst the carnage. Over the driver's seat, I made out Conroy's shoulder.

"Oh, shit, shit, shit," I said, my heart quickening. I reached up, gave Simon's arm a shake, and waited. This time he murmured something, like he did when he talked in his sleep on the bed across from me in the room we shared at Halton House. A wave of relief washed over me for the briefest of moments. What kind of shape was he in? I had no idea. But he was alive. That was all that mattered.

I moved toward Colby and pushed at his shoulder.

"Hey, wake up. Colby—*Colby*," I said. He didn't move, speak, murmur—nothing.

A clump of earth dropped on my head, and a single shaft of bright light lanced down into the van. It was only a few inches around, but it might as well have been a light from heaven. It meant we were near the surface. It beckoned me and I scrambled to the hole with renewed strength and a will not to allow the van to be our steel coffin.

I pulled at the debris, widening the hole, which allowed more sunlight to penetrate the darkness. Then it hit me. Sunrise was around 6 a.m. and we'd been driving Windigo Road at 9 p.m. With it being light outside, it meant that we'd been buried for at least nine hours. Nine hours? Unconscious for nine hours? We could've suffocated to death, I thought.

I recalled the moment before the initial strike, the rumbling, Carol's screech, then the terrifying sounds that I thought would be the last ones I ever heard. But they hadn't been. Beat up, cut, and addled I was. Not dead though. Then something bumped my shoulder and I turned. The whites of Colby's eyes fixed on me from his mud-streaked, panicky face. He didn't speak but looked up at the light. I'd never seen him in such a way. Then he suddenly began to tear at the debris in a frenzy, as if he was single-mindedly focused on getting out and would do whatever it took to do just that. I joined him then. Together we pulled at debris and dug at the dirt like those machines had been doing on Highway 10. Shoulder to shoulder, we widened the hole, better teammates in survival than in basketball. We didn't talk. The only sounds were that incessant electronic pinging and our grunts of heavy breathing from exertion.

Then Colby grabbed a large ball of roots, yanked it a few times until it fell inside, opening a hole wide enough for a person to crawl through, filling the van with fresh air: profusely pure and full of hope. And I knew right then that I would live, that we would live.

"I'm getting out of here," said Colby, his voice shaky.

"What about the others?" I said. "Simon's alive—they might all be alive."

"You're crazy. Let's get out. We can come back for them," he said. He reached up and began to haul himself up through the hole, his feet kicking the air as if he was a swimmer who'd just spotted a shark fin.

Somewhere inside the van a cry erupted. I turned to look around, but couldn't make out anything because Colby's body blocked the light that we'd worked so hard to get. Then another cry, from one of the girls, I was sure. It wasn't a cry for help, more of a primal cry— frightened, confused, searching.

As Colby's feet vanished through the hole, I climbed over the bench seat and the broken molding, groping about in the darkness, following those cries like a rescuer following cries in the rubble after an earthquake. Then a hand seized my wrist and jerked it. A face appeared from the shadows, like a ghostly apparition.

Mud plastered Anna's face. One eye was swollen shut, the other wide and desperate. There wasn't so much as a speck of arrogance left in her. Her world had been completely annihilated. Everything that she thought she knew about the predictability of an affluent life had been robbed by Mother Nature's ferocious and unforgiving natural state of change, a change of whimsy that didn't discriminate by race, religion, or social status. An unstoppable force in its magnitude, which could be avoided if there was enough warning, but never, never stopped. I knew this power intimately, and so too did my mother. She'd spent her life chasing Mother Nature's turmoil—up close and personal—floods, hurricanes, tornados. Until one day, in Oklahoma's Tornado Alley, an F5 that she and her two friends had been chasing swung around 180 degrees and engulfed their truck. I wondered if they'd been in the same predicament as us, entombed in a steel coffin, terrified, hurt, disoriented. Had they been tasting grit and blood in their mouths while looking at death's door, unsure if those moments would be their last, questions filling their minds, wondering if those questions would ever be answered? Who knew? Maybe they'd been unconscious from the onset. That would've been a whole lot better.

"What about Tabby?" said Anna. "What about my uncle?"

Unable to answer because I didn't know, I groped for her seatbelt. Hearing a commotion behind me, I turned back to see Simon's legs disappear through the hole. Anna whimpered as she pushed against the van's paneling, which gave me the bit of room I needed to unbuckle her seatbelt. She fell against my body and clutched me, beginning to sob hysterically.

I pushed her away. "Through the hole," I said.

She fixed on me with her good eye, her expression all terror.

"Go, get out of here," I said, pointing at the light.

She began nodding frantically. She let go of me, and I helped her scramble over the bench seat. Then the van shifted. Maybe only a foot or two, but it shifted.

There was a shadow over the opening, and Simon yelled down, "You need to get out—NOW!"

My heart leapt; sweat ran into my eyes, stinging them. Anna and I moved with a new urgency to the hole where Simon reached down and grabbed one of her outstretched hands. With him pulling and me pushing, Anna went up and through quickly. No sooner had her feet left my sight than the van shifted again, its metal scraping loudly against rock. This time it didn't stop at a mere foot but continued for several. My heart raced crazily.

"Help me," said Tabby. She'd come to and gotten out of her seatbelt on her own. She was wedged in between the front seats frantically shaking her uncle's shoulder.

"We need to hurry," I said, and climbed over the debris toward her. "Move, let me see." I reached around her and stretched over Conroy's body and began to grope for his seatbelt.

The passenger seat was empty, the seatbelt hanging. Carol was gone. The passenger door was gone. The landslide had torn it off. I followed the driver's belt to the button on the buckle, pressed it, and Conroy's body thudded against the warped dash. The engine had been pushed through the firewall, the front end looking like it had collided head on with another vehicle. Then I recalled the tree that had struck the front of the van, right before the lights went dark.

"Where's Carol?" said Tabby.

"Gone."

"Gone where? What are we going to do?"

"Help me," I said.

We each took one of Conroy's arms. We tilted him off the dash, and then dragged and wiggled him out between the seats, his limp body all dead weight. Once in the light, his head rolled to the side to reveal a large gash on his temple. The dried blood coating the right side of his face gave it the look of a zombie mask. I tried to find his pulse, but I couldn't and didn't know if it was just me or because he was dead.

"We need help. Help us," I yelled at the opening. I heard footsteps above me again. A shadow appeared over the hole.

"Hurry," said Simon. "It's going over."

"Over what?" said Tabby.

"Just hurry," he repeated. "Hurry, hurry."

Working together, Tabby and I positioned Conroy directly under the hole, and then we hoisted him up to Simon, who reached down and grabbed his shirt. I held his body up while Tabby moved down to his legs to lift.

She gasped, and said, "Oh my God, his leg—I think it's broken."

It looked like a piece of white plastic was protruding from Conroy's thigh, a broken bone, bloodied and covered in body tissue. I felt sick to my stomach, and I reflexively glanced away, gagging. I took a deep breath and lifted Conroy with every bit of strength that I could muster.

"Push, now, *push*," I yelled to Tabby.

Conroy's head and shoulders rose through the hole, then some of the weight was taken off his body as Simon worked him from his end. Dirt and debris rained down on us. Conroy went through the opening, his bone sickly snagging a few times before his legs and feet exited.

Then the van began shifting again. This time down a slope. It didn't feel like it was going to stop.

"Go, go, go," I said.

Tabby reached up desperately and made a few false grabs before she was successful. She began climbing out. I got under her kicking legs to push her up and caught a heel square in the nose, which caused my eyes to water. The van continued to slide. It was a horrible feeling: closed in and moving God only knew where. Simon's words echoed in my head like a tolling bell—"It's going over"—just as Tabby made it out.

Outside the van the others screamed and yelled, only I couldn't make out what they were saying. Everything seemed to be closing in around me.

Glancing around for anything we might be able to use, unsure if we'd be able to get back inside, I saw Simon's gym bag and Anna's Gucci purse in the debris. I grabbed them by the straps, feeling the van speeding up, scraping against rock. I tossed them through the hole, almost losing my balance as the van continued to slide. And then, as I was about to climb out, I spotted *All the Pretty Horses* near my feet, picked it up, and shoved it into my waistband. Simon's headphones were broken into pieces so I left them. Then I began to scramble through the hole just as the screams and yells outside grew to a fevered pitch: "A cliff, a cliff." The van rotated, picking up even more speed. It made me think of a carnival ride that I'd once been on—what a thing to think!

The light momentarily blinded me, disorienting me, and I quickly blinked away until I could see. The van was sliding toward a canyon as vast as the Grand Canyon. I had only moments to spare. With one final pull, I burst through the hole. I snatched the gym bag and

Gucci purse and leapt from the sliding van to land on the high side of the slope, which was covered in landslide debris. Not looking back, I scrambled and clawed as fast as I could up the slope toward the others, worried I might somehow be swept away.

They were on a rocky portion. Colby and Simon yelled and waved me onwards. The girls huddled beside Conroy's reposed body. As I hustled toward them, I heard the van shear against rock like a death cry before a whooshing sound told me that it had dropped over the edge, an edge I'd almost went over, an edge we all would've gone over if I hadn't come around when I did.

By the time I reached the others, I was sucking wind. They were sorry looking. They reminded me of images that I'd seen of tsunami survivors in *National Geographic*. Their faces were slack and dazed, covered in dirt, their hair wild and tangled, the flesh of their arms scratched and bleeding from hundreds of small cuts and scratches, and their clothes were muddy and torn. An air of shock and bewilderment hung around them like a heavy fog. I figured I looked pretty much the same.

It was eerily silent on the slope. No more sounds came from the canyon, as if the van had dropped into a bottomless void. Maybe it had. The landslide was the size of a soccer field, a patch of earth and rock, broken trees and limbs. It looked like it had fallen from the sky, not formed naturally from coming down the mountainside as landslides do.

"What the hell are those?" said Simon slowly. He was pointing up at the sky across the canyon. Three enormous planets ran in a vertical line. They were peach-colored and each was circled by a set of white rings. The nearest one to the horizon was the largest, the other two smaller as if farther away.

"Planets," whispered Tabby in awe.

"They shouldn't be there," said Simon angrily. "Right?" He looked at me, but I was too glued to them to meet his eyes.

"And those trees look like giant broccoli," said Anna, her voice distant.

Simon said, "We can't see planets like that from . . ."

"From Earth," I said, swallowing.

The fog of shock and bewilderment seemed to thicken, and I became lost for a while as we all gazed around speechlessly at our surroundings. I didn't know how it happened. But the world had somehow changed. We were no longer on our way home to watch Hena give birth to her colt. No longer navigating potholes on Windigo Road. No longer on Mount Romni. No longer in the Pacific Northwest. No longer in the United States of America, Canada no longer an hour to the north.

I turned around. There was a prehistoric-looking forest miles away, with oddly shaped trees (yes, like broccoli) as tall as skyscrapers, their tops brushing the clouds. And above them a gigantic sun bigger than the largest of those three planets—or what looked like a sun— only more reddish than orange, casting everything in a peculiar, fiery glow. Rising into the clouds behind us, there were tiers of rocky, jagged mountains from which a strong breeze carried a raw, earthy smell. Like Mount Romni earlier, only this was stronger, almost palpable. I'd never smelled anything so wild.

Simon was the only one who was standing when I climbed up onto the rock. Colby had sat down. His arms were crossed over his knees and he was slumped forward as if he'd given in to exhaustion, as if the accident and escape had robbed him of all his energy. The girls were still huddled against Conroy, one on either side of him.

"Grabbed what I could," I said, tossing the bag and purse onto the rock.

"Man, lucky you didn't go over," said Colby.

I was about to call him out for leaving me—call him a coward or chickenshit—but didn't think it was the time or place. Instead I just huffed, turned away. Disgusted. Pissed off.

"We're all lucky," said Simon.

"What about Carol?" said Anna, grabbing her purse.

I faced the debris. Conroy, pale and trembling, propped up on his elbow to speak: "She's gone."

"What do you mean gone?" said Anna, her voice cracking.

"From the van," he said hoarsely. "Ejected from the van."

"Oh my God," said Anna. She put her shaky hand to her mouth, stifling a sob.

"Her door was missing," said Tabby, her voice tremulous. Both girls began to cry and reached for their uncle to embrace him in a hug.

"She didn't have her seatbelt on," I said, in a faraway voice that didn't sound like my own. "It was just hanging there."

Colby looked between his legs like he was searching the bottom of a well, shook his head, and said, "And she's always telling us to buckle up."

7

Vince had shown me how to splint a leg once, after I brought home a wild bunny, which I'd found the neighbor's fat farm cat pawing at the edge of the north hayfield, near a copse of aspens. I didn't intervene right away. At first, I watched what I'd been taught was a natural cycle of life, a predator that had caught its prey, but then there'd been a stirring in me, in my guts, and I quickly realized I couldn't allow him to continue. Maybe it had been the way he was toying with the bunny, swatting it back and forth, then bringing his paw down like a hammer. I couldn't sit idly by and allow it to be killed and eaten, no matter how much of a natural cycle of life it was.

I'd been carrying a pocket full of flat quarter-sized stones that I picked out of a wash that ran through the field. (I used to zing them at trees and fence-posts, that sort of thing, and got pretty good at it.) I let one fly at the cat's rump, not enough to hurt him, just enough to send it darting into the aspens.

The bunny crawled feebly away as I approached, its eyes wide, body heaving, but only made it a few feet or so before stopping. Its left front leg splayed at an odd angle. I whispered soothingly to it like I did with the horses and cows, coming around so my shadow wouldn't fall overtop and scare it. I gently slid my hands under the furry body, cradled it to my chest. The legs kicked a few times until I began to rub its back.

Like the bunny was a baby in my arms, I carried it back to the big shop beside the house where Vince was sharpening a chainsaw with a file. He told me that I should've left it out in the field, and then he went back to work. I looked down at the furry body in my arms and turned to trudge off, my shoulders slumped, more than a little disappointed.

"Bring him over to the workbench," sighed Vince. "I got something that might help."

"How do you know it's a he?" I said, turning around, uplifted. He'd only seen it from ten feet away.

"You ask all the tough questions, you know that, Tanner," he said. "Here, put him down on this horse blanket. I'll show you how to make a splint. You never know, you might need to make one someday."

There on that mountain slope, far, far away from Vince's workshop or a hospital or any civilization, it seemed that the "someday" Vince spoke of had arrived. The more I gazed around, the more I felt like we'd traveled back in time to a prehistoric world, untouched by humankind's hand. And there I was, about to make a splint.

Simon and I silently headed down to the debris field and began combing through it, pretending not to search for Carol's remains while we searched for splint material. As we did, the others stayed sitting on the rock, staring vacantly at us.

I found a large branch from a maple tree with smaller branches shooting off, which must've come along with us because there were no maple trees anywhere in sight. I broke off two of the thinner, straighter branches, and gave one to Simon. We each denuded them as we hiked back up the slope to rejoin the others.

When I told Conroy we wanted to splint his leg, he agreed, but said we first needed to set the bone properly, which he would help us do. Grimacing, Conroy slowly reached into his pocket and took out the Swiss Army knife that he always carried with him.

Anna and Tabby moved away, giving us room. Conroy handed me the knife and told me to cut the cargo pants from the hip down, so I opened the blade and carefully made a small cut and ran the blade all the way down through the cuff of his pants.

Conroy's face was a mask of pain; every little movement must've hurt like hell. A jagged piece of his femur protruded from his flesh, looking worse out in the daylight than it had in the van. Anna groaned and turned away. Tabby shook her hands in the air like the sight of it had twanged her nerves.

Simon took a bottle of water out of his gym bag. He began to slowly pour it on the wound, washing away the congealed blood. It mingled with the water, turning it a roseate color, which pooled on the rock under Conroy's leg. The wound was ugly, and I knew setting the bone would be excruciatingly painful. There was no doubt about that, and no way around it.

Anna and Tabby gave us some more room. Colby got up and began to limp down to the debris.

"Where are you going?" I said.

"I ain't watching this," he said over his shoulder.

"Don't go too far," I said.

"Who made you big kahuna?"

"Boys, you need to close this wound up," said Conroy. His words were like an order from a man who was used to leading others into dangerous situations, like he had as a Marine sergeant in Iraq. I'd seen his medals, the photos in his album. And I'd even heard a few stories when two vets who he'd served with visited Halton House one Saturday afternoon a few months back—Big Trudgoen with his icy blue eyes and Ruiz with his prosthetic arm and shrapnel-scarred face. Conroy's face was getting paler by the moment. Blood vessels in his right eye had ruptured, leaving it almost completely red. I'd never seen anyone in such rough shape. The lower half of his leg still lay at its odd angle, splayed out from his body, which made me think again of that bunny's leg.

"I've never done anything like this before," said Simon, voice tiny.

"You'll be fine," whispered Conroy, then shut his eyes and fell back to lie motionless.

Simon looked panicked. "Oh, shit—did he just . . ."

"Passed out," I said.

I handed the knife to Tabby, then wiped sweat from my eye. "Tabby, help Anna cut the towel into strips," I said.

Anna picked up the towel off Simon's gym bag.

"Hope you washed that thing?" I said.

Simon and I both kneeled on either side of his broken leg. "Okay, move his calf to the left until I tell you to stop," I said.

"Ugh, this is way ugly," said Simon, glancing away.

"If we don't do this, he might lose his leg," I said. "Might even die."

Simon gingerly took hold of Conroy's calf.

As soon as I rested my hands on it, I felt spasms pulsing through his leg like electric currents were zapping him. I tightened my hold in hopes to lessen them, but it didn't work. They only increased.

I looked at Simon and said, "Okay, on three." He gave a nod. On three we started to delicately shift his calf to the left, blood dribbling from the wound. Conroy grunted in unconscious stupor and his fingertips reflexively raked the rock. The bone slowly sunk back into the purplish flesh as we straightened his leg until it was in line with his thigh.

Without even having to ask her for them, Tabby handed us the denuded branches that she'd cleaned off with water. I placed one on either side of his leg.

Simon and I then proceeded to tie them tightly into place with strips of towel.

When we finished, Conroy was still unconsciousness. Far from ideal, best we could do.

"How'd you learn how to do that?" asked Anna, a bit of awe in her voice. "I mean, I took Level One First Aid, but I never learned anything like this."

"On the farm," I said.

Colby climbed onto the rock, carrying a long stick. When he saw the splint, he said, "Can't just leave it like that."

"It's all we can do right now," I said, "until we find a . . ."

"A *what*? A hospital? Ain't no hospital, man. Look around," he said, whirling around dramatically in a circle. "We're a long, long way from home. Long way—you better believe that."

"Enough with the hysterics," snapped Simon.

"I'm being real, that's all," said Colby.

"There's no one going to show up, is there?" said Anna.

"See, see what you did?" said Simon.

"There's got to be people around here somewhere," said Tabby, turning toward the forest.

Everyone became gravely silent as Anna searched our faces for support. I knew Colby was right. I hated it. But he was right. I thought everyone else must know, too, but then I watched enough TV to know that shock does strange things to people.

"What about him?" said Anna, squeezing her uncle's hand.

Tabby rubbed Conroy's arm, but he didn't budge or even make a peep. And I thought back to the time I crashed my dirt bike and broke my arm, and how my entire body felt paralyzed. I figured that was how Conroy would feel for a little while. And my broken arm hadn't been nearly as bad a break as Conroy's leg.

"I don't think anyone's coming, Anna," I said. "Even if they do . . ." I looked away.

"What's that mean?" said Anna, searching faces again.

"That means the locals might not be friendly," said Colby. "Might be some mean, nasty types. Just like in *King Kong*. Real savages."

"Okay, so what then?" said Tabby. "What do we do?"

No one answered.

"Do you have your phone?" I said.

Anna rooted through her purse. "Yes, yes. It's still on. Everything else fell out except the phone." She pulled out her iPhone and held it up like it was some large, precious jewel, its silver casing glinting in the peculiar red sun.

"That's just great," said Colby, slapping his thighs, "we gonna die while listening to crappy retro."

"Oh, and this," added Anna, and lifted out one of her fruit-and-nut bars.

"Are you getting a signal?" I said, a spark of hope lifting my spirits.

Shaking her head, she said, "No, no, nothing."

"Your phone ain't gonna work here," said Colby, scoffing.

A bluff nosed above a patch of gnarly trees a ways up the mountainside. "See that rock bluff up there? Maybe we can pick up a signal on your phone."

"I say we all stay right here," said Colby, pouring some water on a piece of towel. "Staying put is what you're supposed to do." He began to wipe his Nikes clean.

"Great way to ration the water," said Simon. "Carol's dead. We're lost. And you're cleaning your prized fucking shoes!"

"What do you want me to do, man? Huh. You tell me 'cause I got no idea."

"I think Colby's right," said Anna.

"You just said yourself we're a long way from home. Feel that chill in the air," I said. The air had grown noticeably cooler over the last hour. "The sun's dropping and we're on the slope of a mountain. It's going to get colder. We need to find shelter. And we still need to build a stretcher."

"Build a stretcher?" said Colby. "Ain't nothing to build a stretcher with."

"Why do you always have to be so pessimistic?" said Tabby.

"You mean realistic—big difference—and why you got to cut your hair like a boy?" He said, pointing the stick at her head.

"Screw you, jackass," said Tabby. "It's called a gamine cut."

"There's material up there," I said, nodding to the mountain. "We can get what we need and check for a signal at the same time. But we need to move now."

"He's right," said Conroy, his voice low and weak. He'd come to and propped up on his elbows again. He looked even rougher than before, which I would've thought impossible if I hadn't been seeing it with my own two eyes.

Anna leaned over and hugged his shoulders. Tabby motioned for the bottle of water and Colby handed it to her. She poured some into his mouth, water running down his chin. Conroy turned one way and then the other as if he was trying to get his bearings.

I could tell he was lost. He had no idea what to do. Would anybody? One thing he did do, though, was remain calm and composed. It was a quality that I admired greatly. My uncle Hanker had that way about him also. From the stories I'd heard about my father, he had it too. I figured the military instilled that in them, or maybe some were simply born with it, like a person inherited a trait or an eye color from their ancestors.

Conroy asked Anna to try 911 on her iPhone. Nothing. He asked her to try text messaging. Still nothing. Finally, he asked her to try the Internet. She tried for a minute while we all watched anxiously, but again there was nothing. He asked us to all gather around. We formed a semi-circle with those three strange planets as a backdrop. "I don't know what happened or where we are," he said. "But you've all handled this remarkably well."

"None of this makes sense," said Anna, her voice wavering.

"No, no, I'm not about to lie and say it does," he said. "We're going to need to work together if we want to make it out of this."

Colby jumped up, tossed his arms in frustration, and thrust the stick up at the planets—angrily and defiantly—like the world had been unfair and he wasn't prepared to take it anymore. "Get home," he said. "Any of you seen planets like that before?"

"Saturn has rings around it," said Simon. "And also Uranus, or maybe it's Neptune."

"Yeah, yeah, he's right. Saturn does have rings," said Anna, lifting her head from her uncle's shoulder with a wild, false look of hope on her face. Tears had streaked channels on her muddy cheeks.

"None of it matters right now. We need to find shelter—*yesterday*," I said louder and more forcefully than I'd intended. As though to bolster my point, a stiff gust suddenly swept down the mountain, raising goosebumps on my arms. "That sun'll be gone in a few hours."

"Always trying to be the shot caller," said Colby, slashing the stick back and forth in the air.

"*Enough*," said Conroy. "Tanner's right. The temperature will continue to drop. We need to find shelter or we risk hypothermia."

"We might be popsicles before morning," said Simon. He picked up two rocks and swiped them together a few times. If he was trying for a spark, he didn't have any luck.

Conroy turned to me and nodded toward the mountain. "How long you figure to climb to that bluff?"

I thought about it a moment, and then said, "Maybe an hour. Less to come back."

"Okay, good, good," said Conroy weakly. "Let's try for a signal before we head to the forest. Might not get another chance."

"I'll build a stretcher," I said, and then looked at the others. "We'll build a stretcher."

Colby shook his head, like he thought it all bad.

"I'll go with him," said Simon. He tossed the rocks down and stood up.

Anna handed me her iPhone. I put it in the pocket of my sweatpants. "Here, take this too," said Anna, giving the fruit-and-nut bar to Simon. "You might need it."

"I ain't letting you two meatballs go by yourselves," said Colby. He turned and strode past us and began up the slope. "Well, we doing this?" he yelled over his shoulder.

"What about your shoes?" said Simon after Colby.

Colby flipped him the bird and kept walking.

I was about to say the three of us should stick together when Conroy shook his head tiredly, like he didn't want me to try to argue a point with Colby, then laid back again and shut his eyes.

"Hang on, one of you should stay with us," said Anna desperately.

"I can go with you, Tanner," said Tabby, stepping forward. She was serious. Simon shrugged his shoulders like he was saying why not. He tossed the fruit-and-nut bar to Tabby and gave me his gym bag with the water bottle inside.

Anna told us to be careful. Without another word, Tabby and I began to follow Colby up the grassy slope. He hadn't slowed his step whatsoever, his head tilted back in that defiant way of his. Only this time it was directed at the mountain as if it had been solely responsible for our misfortune. And that was how we started off.

8

We passed through a field of long, wispy grass billowing in the wind, and wild flowers with bright orange buds rising from the center and pointy narrow leaves on their stalks. The field gave way to fragmented boulders that looked as if they'd sheared from higher up some time ago and slid or tumbled down the mountain before coming to rest. We came to a copse of gnarly, fir-like trees—twenty, thirty feet tall—deformed by a wind we'd yet to feel. Before we entered, I stole a glance down the slope. Anna and Simon both waved like they'd been waiting for us to look at them. I waved back before carrying on.

"Hey, look what I got here," said Colby. "My man's favorite pet." He whirled around, holding a small black snake by the tail. It hissed and writhed and tried to twist up and bite his hand. I backed up a few steps. My stomach knotted; beads of cold sweat formed on my forehead. Snakes! Creepy. Slippery. I hated snakes, had ever since two water moccasins bit my hand when I was ten, and I had to be rushed to the ER for a shot of anti-venom. My whole hand and forearm had swollen up like a watermelon. Colby knew of my phobia. I'd shared the story with both him and Simon during our last trip to the pet store, to buy fish food for the Oscars at Halton House.

"Better put it down. Could be highly venomous. Even deadly venomous," said Tabby, deathly serious.

"Piddly little sucker like this," said Colby. He swung it up through the air.

"Berg adders are only ten inches long. Their venom can drop an elephant," she said.

57

"Oh, yeah, how you know?" said Colby, squinted-eyed.

"One of the benefits of having an egghead sister, I guess."

Colby flung the snake toward a pile of rocks. As soon as it hit the ground, it tried to slither out of sight, but a black plant with a head the size and shape of a football bobbed down and gobbled it up, sucking its tail up like a spaghetti string.

"What was that?" said Tabby, mystified.

"I don't know, but they're everywhere," I said. The same plants—thin foot-long stocks and big bulbous heads—spotted the entire mountainside.

"Man, just a big old flytrap," said Colby. Acting nonchalant, all cool-like, he turned and resumed hiking up the trail.

"Only ten inches and drops an elephant?" I whispered.

"No," whispered Tabby out of the corner of her mouth, "more like twenty-five to thirty-five inches. And those are definitely not just flytraps."

We went to catch up with Colby, more mindful of our surroundings.

The three of us wended through rocks and trees, slowly ascending the mountainside up no defined path, occasionally stopping to drink water from the bottle. Eventually we came to a steeper portion where a path zigzagged back and forth like one of those mountain goat paths that I'd seen in Montana's high country. Colby stopped and leaned against a tree, breathing heavily, and used his shirt to wipe sweat from his face. He waved for us to pass, to take the lead.

With the line of sight cut, and the sun dipping quicker than I'd expected, an uneasy feeling overcame me. I told Tabby and Colby that we needed to pick up the pace, and so we did. We began to hike much faster. About three quarters of the way up, loose rock slid down the mountainside off to our right, echoing, and blooming dust, which swept out over the valley. A shaggy black animal scrambled along one of the lower paths.

"See that?" I said.

"What is it?" said Tabby.

"I don't know," I said, and then on second thought, loud enough so Colby could hear: "Maybe a giant grizzly out looking for dinner." I grinned mischievously at Tabby and winked. We left Colby leaning against a tree, catching his breath, and staring at the clump of boulders into which the animal had disappeared. He'd made his fear of bears well known. And I thought what better time to even the score.

A few seconds later, I heard him rushing after us.

It wasn't long before we ended up on one of the paths that ran directly underneath the bluff. Every ten or so seconds, I'd turn back in hopes of getting a line of sight on the others below, but I never did. I caught myself thinking of all the times I'd been out hiking in Montana with no destination in mind, a chance to be free of everything, everyone. During those times, I never felt so free, never felt so alive. But then this wasn't Montana.

No more shaggy animals appeared on the mountain as we neared the bluff, which rose higher than I'd originally thought. A good fifty or sixty feet at least.

When we got there, I inspected one side and then the other while Tabby and Colby sat down to rest. There was no easy way up. Both sides rose steeply with only loose slate on the slope, and tiny scrub trees growing here and there.

"Who's going up?" said Colby.

I could tell by the way he said it that he didn't want to go any farther. In the sky to the left, I spotted two large brown birds, circling high above like the eagles that I used to watch in Montana. The two were joined by a third, and then another one appeared out over the forest, followed by three more. They were so high up that it was difficult to make out their features.

"Nothing about this looks normal," said Colby. "And my Aunty Watts got a whole stack of *National Geographic.*"

"Let's give it a shot, and start back down," said Tabby.

"Who's going up?" said Colby again.

They both stared at me.

"I guess I am," I said.

"I'll go with you," said Tabby.

"No, it's better if I go by myself," I continued. "If I stay tight along the side, I should be able to use those little trees to climb up."

"How long have we been gone?" said Tabby.

"I don't know," said Colby. "I can't believe ain't none of us got a watch."

"Everyone relies on handheld devices now," said Tabby.

"Hour and a half," I said uneasily, knowing we'd been longer than predicted. "We've been gone about an hour and a half." I handed Tabby Simon's gym bag.

She took out the water bottle and tried to hand it to me. There was only a bit left, a few mouthfuls at most. I waved her off and then rounded the corner to begin my climb.

It was steeper than it first looked and the loose slate kept slipping underfoot. For every four steps up, there were two back. I picked my way along, using fissures in the bluff and small trees for handholds. It took me about ten minutes or so to reach the top. Longer than I'd hoped. By the time I did, my fingers were raw; sweat stung my eyes. I walked out to the end, the wind tousling my hair, drying the sweat on my face and body. What lay before me was unlike anything my imagination could fathom.

9

A vastness stretched out in every direction. To the right lay the forest of massive broccoli trees, some tops lost in the clouds. Where the canyon met the forest, a plume of mist swirled up from a waterfall. Straight ahead and to the left the plains sprawled forever on the horizon. The strange planets above. Everything was huge and weird, almost palpable with alien-like vibrancy and smells.

A large herd of animals grazed on the other side of the chasm, directly across from where the van had dropped off. There must've been hundreds of them—tan animals that I thought might've been deer, only they didn't have antlers. Conroy and the others were still out of sight. It would've made me feel more comfortable seeing them there, being able to give them a wave and get one in return.

Treetops just off the bluff obscured Tabby and Colby from view. Behind me the mountainside rose up like steps leading to Mount Olympus and those ancient gods that I'd been reading about my entire life. I wondered if the world we now found ourselves in possessed its own myths and legends, heroes and monsters, gods from the past who haunted the present and epic battles between good and evil.

I removed Anna's iPhone from my pocket and lifted it up, hoping for a signal to appear on the screen. Instead, I was greeted by a photo of Anna wearing sunglasses, looking far older than her seventeen years. There was no signal. Nothing. I lifted it higher. I tried turning in a circle, then waving it about, still nothing. I accessed her text messages. There were dozens of outgoing ones to the same person—Rick. I opened one message: *Can't do this alone. It's your baby too. Please call or txt me,* and then another: *Please call me. I need to talk.*

Suddenly a shrill cry resounded across the valley and up the mountainside. One of those giant birds dove toward the herd of grazing animals on the plain, like I'd seen those eagles do when diving after salmon in rivers. As it neared the earth, its wings swept out to slow its descent. There was a flash of yellow talons. Then with pinpoint accuracy the bird snatched one of the animals. With a powerful beating of wings, it rose back up into the sky. Two more birds dove at the herd, both striking their targets. A shadow landed on my face. Another bird flew directly overhead and out over the slope. I slid Anna's iPhone back into my pocket, my heart quickening.

Another shaggy black animal scrambled along one of the paths halfway down the mountainside, though I couldn't tell if it was the same one from earlier. The bird that had just flown overhead released a shrill cry, then dove. A moment later it struck the animal, which erupted in loud squeals. And it was only then I realized how enormous those birds were, the size of small private jets.

Then suddenly all the other birds began to dive on the herd like someone had rung a dinner bell. A warmth bloomed on my chest, and I patted the medicine pouch, feeling heat coming from inside.

The hairs on my neck and arms stood on end before a mighty gust of wind buffeted my back, sending dust and debris swirling into the air. A shrill cry pierced my eardrums. Without a second thought, I bolted forward with six bounds and leapt off the edge toward the treetops. Dropping a good ways, I snagged a tangle of branches in an attempt to stop my descent, or at least slow it. Branches tore and clawed at me as I fell through the trees. A heavy thud sounded behind me, followed by a broken squawk, then wings flapped overhead.

The underside of my arms struck a thick lower branch. My momentum swung me off and I fell the last bit to strike the rocky ground on my hands and knees beside Colby and Tabby. They both helped me to my feet.

The bird I'd narrowly escaped from flew out over the slope toward the canyon, herky-jerky, dipping and rising. Hitting the bluff must've rung its bell pretty good. If it'd been me instead of the bluff, my back would've snapped like a piece of dry kindling. The bird assumed a glide for a moment, but then descended, its wings beating feebly, uselessly. It released a strangled cry, which tore across the valley, before dropping into the canyon's maw, vanishing like our van.

"Heard the scream, man. Thought you was bird food," said Colby.

"Are you all right?" said Tabby.

My heart thundered like a stampede of wild horses across an open plain, leaving me breathless, my hands shaking. "No reception," I said between breaths.

"What'd I tell you?" said Colby.

"What about the others?" said Tabby. "Did you see the others?"

Her words hit me like a blow—Conroy and the others. With nowhere to hide, they were exposed on the lower slope. We'd been worried about the temperature, but how could we have imagined there'd be a flock of voracious, man-eating birds hunting for dinner.

In the distance, over the plain, I could make out at least a dozen more. Most had silhouetted shapes hanging from their talons, a few carrying nothing. We moved around and tried to peer through the trees to get a line of sight on the others. It was no use. So I tore off down the path without another word, my bad knee aching, Colby and Tabby right on my heels.

We ran and slid down the zigzagging paths, kicking up dust, which blew out over the slope. Every time I neared a copse of trees, I slowed down in fear of striking a trunk and weaved my way through, always keeping an eye to the sky, and then took off on another stretch of path to the next copse. While we repeated this over and over, how many times I don't know, I thought how stupid we'd been to leave Conroy and the others behind like that, alone on the slope with no protection. I knew Anna and Simon didn't have the strength to move Conroy any great distance by themselves. It just wasn't physically possible. I tried to recall if one of those silhouettes in the birds' talons had been a human form, or if maybe there'd been human screams mixed in with the wind and cries. I couldn't say, but in twenty minutes I'd have my answer.

10

We stood there catching our breath on the rock where we'd left the others just over two hours ago. No one was there. There was no Gucci purse, no pieces of towel, nothing except for remnants of dried blood from when we'd rinsed Conroy's wound before splinting his leg.

"Oh, nononono, not like this. No way, man," said Colby. "No fucking way."

Tabby did a three-sixty, scanning the land. Behind us only a fingernail of that massive red sun remained over the mountains, setting the valley afire in an eerie red glow. Soon it would dip out of sight, and then we'd experience our first night on that new world. I wondered what night had in store for us, besides the ever-increasing cold.

Out of the corner of my eye, I saw something that I'd missed on first inspection, or maybe it was the way the light had slightly changed. The waist-high grass had been disturbed. A swath about three feet wide ran from the rock all the way to the forest.

"Look," I said, pointing at the grass. "They went to the forest."

"Oh, yeah," said Tabby. "There it is, sure."

"Regular bush boy you are," said Colby. "But how'd they move him all that way by themselves?"

Leaping off the rock, not wanting to waste time, I said, "Let's go find out." As I waded through the waist-high grass, following the trail, I again tried to picture Anna and Simon lifting and hauling Conroy to the forest. Simon was wiry, strong for his size, but not strong enough. I couldn't see it. I'd learned the heft of heavy weight and a person's capability lifting it while living at Whispering Cedars, carrying around things like bags of fertilizer, hay bales, newborn calves, and tractor parts. There was no way they could've moved him that distance. But somehow they'd all moved.

No sooner had we set off than the sun's red glow changed to a violet color, bathing the landscape in an odd kind of twilight unlike anything I'd ever seen. And the closer we got to those broccoli-shaped trees, the larger they seemed to be. I began to hear strange sounds, wilder than anything I'd ever heard before—frenzied croaks, staccato clicks, rapid flaps and flutters, as though an alien nature chorus had been unleashed.

We paused at the edge of the forest. I looked up, stunned. The tree trunks were as big around as houses and they seemed to rise for thousands of feet. The air was humid. Birds—regular sized—circled and weaved around the heights, their songs echoing strangely in the natural cathedral. A trail of matted brown needles, some disturbed, led into the forest and wended through the trunks until it vanished.

"Look at the way the needles are kicked up," I said. "Could've been the others." I found myself second-guessing the seriousness of Conroy's injury, thinking maybe it wasn't as bad as we'd originally thought. Then the image of that protruding bone from his torn flesh came back to me. It was bad, very bad.

"Should we call out?" said Tabby.

"I don't know," I said.

"What if we call out and . . . something calls back?" said Colby uncertainly.

"Um, that's the point, isn't it?" said Tabby.

"I mean, what if something else besides the others calls back?" said Colby.

"Like what?" said Tabby, and after a brief pause: "Oh, I see what you mean."

They were nervous, hesitant to enter the forest, to cross the threshold into another place on that strange new world. What dwelled inside? Who knew? We'd almost been devoured by giant birds. What waited for us inside the forest? Colby was right. What if something else did hear our calls and decided to come and investigate? What if it was something that we didn't want to meet face to face? What then? I felt terribly vulnerable standing there, shaking, wondering.

"You got a point," I said. I looked from Colby to Tabby. "I say we follow the trail, be quiet, keep our eyes open. I doubt they went that far."

Colby nodded, but I could tell he didn't really want to go any farther.

"Sounds good to me," said Tabby.

They both just stared at me like they were waiting for me to say more. We'd been here before. The first step would be mine. I gave my head a shake, smiled to myself, and entered the forest, leading the way on the trail. I felt like an ant among those trees—an ant followed by two other ants. As we got deeper into the forest, the trees and foliage acted as a windbreak against the mountain breeze that we'd been experiencing since we first arrived, and my goosebumps subsided. The trail of disturbed needles carried on, and so did we.

Between the bark on the trees were cracks wide enough a person could hide in, or an animal. In some of the trunks were cavernous holes big enough to drive a Chevy pickup into. I couldn't figure out what was making those wild sounds, nor was I about to go traipsing off the trail to find out. About twenty minutes in, a loud crash echoed throughout the forest, then somewhere a stampede began, rumbling the ground underfoot. We stopped dead in our tracks and looked around. We couldn't make out from which direction it'd originated, which direction it was heading. The forest's canopy made every sound spooky, made echoes that carried on everywhere. We dashed to the edge of the trail and hunched down behind fern leaves the size of cars, trying to figure out whether we were in danger or not. Gradually the stampede faded off. We stood and started to make our way along the trail again, this time more warily, following those disturbed needles.

To be honest, at that point, I began to have doubts. What if the others had been snatched by the birds? What if something else was responsible for the swath in the grass, for disturbing the needles? What if it had been some kind of animal? At Whispering Cedars, old ranch hand Jerry had shown me the basics a few times of how to spot cow track, and also predator tracks like wolves and bears and wild cats that might be stalking the ranch's livestock. But that was it. I was no expert. Far from it. As we carried on, it began to feel like blind faith. But what were our options? Go back and freeze to death on the slope? Even if we made it through the night, then what? Be awoken at dawn by those giant birds screaming down for breakfast? And what if Conroy and the others needed us, needed our help? I didn't know what Tabby and Colby were thinking. I didn't ask. I was dog-tired, and so I was sure they were, too.

Half an hour passed, then one hour, and still the trail went on. At one point, I heard a turbulent fluttering overhead. As I stared up, my imagination conjured up a giant black bat with red eyes chasing insects. But how big, this bat? If the birds were any gauge, the bats would be freakishly big. But like that stampede we'd heard earlier, the fluttering soon faded off, leaving us with those other sounds we'd been hearing since we entered the forest. Leaving us with louder heartbeats.

11

The trail eventually narrowed and began running alongside a swiftly moving river, forty feet or so wide. We followed it until we arrived at a place where the trail merged with the water. The bank sloped down, like a fisherman's spot or where someone would launch a small boat. We went to the river's edge. The stars were casting their glittering wishes upon the surface. A melodic sound filled the night. On the side of the trees facing the river, moss-like patches of long red grass brushed back and forth in the breeze, sounding like harps. My skin tingled, causing a shiver to run through my body. It would've been beautiful, there on the bank, if there weren't so many unknowns, questions unanswered, all itching at my mind.

Tabby knelt down. "Let's stop here a minute," she said. She cupped a handful of water to her mouth.

"Wait a second," I said "You don't know if it's safe to drink."

She turned and gave me a skeptical look.

"I'm serious," I said.

"Looks fine to me, like momma's milk," said Colby, kneeling down beside Tabby. He quickly scooped a handful to his mouth and began rinsing it around exaggeratedly. "Mmmm, tastes like it too," he said.

I joined them at the river's edge, slaking my thirst with fresh, cold water as pure as any mountain spring in the Montana countryside. I hadn't realized just how thirsty I'd been. We gulped like parched horses at the trough, splashing water on our faces and necks, washing away the sweat and grime we'd yet to cleanse ourselves of. And when we had our fill, we just sat there, bellies full. Then I remembered the heat from the pouch. I pulled it out from around my neck, and dumped the stone out into my hand. It was exactly as I remembered—tiny, smooth, shiny, black. There was no heat coming from it, as there had been right before the bird dove at me.

Tabby nudged my arm. She gave a sneaky smile and gestured to Colby who was using a piece of fern to wipe clean his Nikes. I couldn't help but shake my head.

Suddenly a splash sounded upriver, followed by another and another. I lifted my head up to look but could only see the orangey light from the planets, similar to moonlight, reflecting on the river's surface. The splashing became a steady rhythm, growing louder by the second, as if a rain cloud had opened up above the river and was moving toward us while dropping huge raindrops.

"What is that?" said Tabby.

"Don't know, but it's heading our way," said Colby.

I stood up from where I'd been sitting and backed away from the bank, the others doing the same. Then I saw it, or should say them. Fish, tiny fish no bigger than minnows coming toward us, leaping ten, fifteen feet in the air, and then diving. Hundreds of them, maybe even thousands, their scales glistening silver in the moony light as they arced through the sky. We reflexively backed away a bit farther, watching in wonder as a steady stream passed us for what seemed like a minute. I don't think any of us knew what to make of it. I sure didn't. Then just as quickly as they came, they went, the splashes fading off downriver.

"Whatcha think they gonna do at that waterfall?" said Colby.

"Probably fly," said Tabby.

"Or maybe sprout legs and run off into the forest," I said.

We all laughed. Even with everything that had happened, we were still able to laugh. And it felt good, really good.

Tabby dug into Simon's gym bag and removed the water bottle and went to the edge to fill it. A raccoon scurried from the undergrowth and stopped behind her. It paused, turned first to Tabby, and then to Colby and me, fixing on us with its tiny black eyes, before making a grunting noise. Three baby coons that couldn't have been more than a few months old, bounded to catch up, playfully bouncing into one another as if they were having a good old time. When the brood was behind their mother, she led them down to the riverbank where they scurried upriver along its edge.

"Raccoons?" said Colby. No sooner had the words left his mouth, than I saw it emerge silently from the forest. Graceful, its white hide a sheen, a long ivory spire protruding from its forehead. A unicorn colt, just like the kind I'd heard about in fables and myths since I could remember, stood right there in front of us. Statuesque.

Tabby and Colby looked at me, both their faces slack, mouths hanging open farther than I thought possible. The unicorn went down to the river and sniffed the water. When he lowered his head to take a drink, another unicorn emerged from the forest. This one was larger. It was a mare. Neighing loudly, she trotted over to her colt and nudged him aside with her head. She sniffed the water herself, like she was inspecting it. She lifted her head and whinnied, then she cautiously started to drink. The colt joined his mother, neither paying any attention to us.

"Unicorns?" whispered Colby reverently.

"Like we don't exist," whispered Tabby.

"They aren't afraid," I whispered. "Either never seen people or the ones they've seen treated them kindly. The deer, raccoons, and even skunks are like that around Whispering Cedars. They'd come right up to me and eat out of my hand."

"That's what animals were like in North America before Europeans arrived," said Tabby. She took a few steps toward the unicorn mare. She slowly reached out. Only when she brushed her fingertips along the mare's neck did the mare lift her head to look, with a honey-colored eye, before lowering it again to continue drinking.

In that moment, the direness of our situation seemed to diminish, and our surroundings no longer felt so alien and bizarre, as though the forest's inhabitants had come out to greet us, letting us know there was nothing to be afraid of. I felt calm, even safe, for the first time since we arrived on that strange new world. Then something caught my eye. A flicker of light a ways off through the trees. I waited for it to vanish, but it continued to glow, only broken intermittently by the forest's undergrowth.

"Hey, look, a light upriver," I whispered, as if saying it any louder might cause it to disappear.

Tabby stopped petting the mare, and the two unicorns walked off down the bank as the raccoons had done moments before. All three of us fixed on the light.

"Whatcha think it is?" whispered Colby.

"Maybe the others," whispered Tabby.

"We don't know who it is," I whispered. It could've been the others, which would've made the most sense, but then it was on the other side of the river. Not only that, but by that point not a whole lot was making sense. That safe feeling began to dissipate. Tabby stepped away from the bank, slung the gym bag over her shoulder, readying to go. The light began to move around.

My mind associated it with something that I'd seen before. At first, I thought it might've been a sparkler like people used on the Fourth of July. But then it wasn't shooting off like a sparkler. I thought maybe a glow stick? But then it was small multiple lights clustered together, like a bunch of glowing grapes. I looked at the bank. A part of me wanted to stay right there for the night, wake up to that reddish sun beaming down on me in morning. Guilt washed over me then at even considering not continuing our search for the others. Like the guilt that I'd felt when I saw the fear on the faces of all those customers and employees at the banks Uncle Hanker and I had robbed. Like the guilt I still felt when I thought about them. We'd been wearing ball caps and bandanas over our faces, just like Colby had said, like two Wild West outlaws, Uncle Hanker waving around his chrome .38 Smith & Wesson, and me with brown canvas bags full of bills. All of it had been seared into me with a red-hot brand, so I would never forget what I'd done. If my heart and soul could be seen, people never would either.

Conroy and the others were still out there somewhere, frightened, hurt, and alone, without shelter. It could've been one of them with the light, trying to signal for help, hoping we'd spot them, but then I was certain they didn't have anything like that with them. Or did they?

"That's got to be at least a mile off," I said.

"Just making plain old circles," said Colby.

Tabby and Colby came over to my side and together we watched. There was definitely a pattern. A high circle, then a low one. Over and over again.

"We got to check. We got make sure, right?" said Tabby.

"Yes, we do," I said.

"I don't like it, something don't feel right," said Colby.

"We'll sneak up and find out what it is," I said. "If it's not them, we'll vamoose."

"They ain't got nothing makes that kind of light," said Colby. "Anna's lighter don't do that."

"Lighter?" I said.

"She always slinking off to smoke," he said. "You don't know?"

"She smokes?" I said.

"Lots you don't know 'bout her, man," said Colby. "Betcha lots none of us knows 'bout her.

"Yeah, betcha there's a lot we don't know about you," said Tabby.

I thought of the text messages on the iPhone, figured maybe Colby was right, for once. I wondered if Tabby knew her sister was pregnant. "Well, let's check this out," I said.

"We fine right here for now. We keep going farther we might end up lost," said Colby, trace of fear in his voice.

Tabby and I looked at each other. Colby stared at us hoping he'd get us to change our minds.

"We need to," I said. "Just to be sure."

"Okay, shot caller, then lead the way," said Colby.

12

I led the way again, almost at a march, irked by Colby's selfish attitude. But then it was Colby, not the Dalai Lama or Bill Gates or Warren Buffet. With nightfall fully upon us, and the canopy blocking the moony light, the disturbed needles were becoming more difficult to make out. After a few minutes back on the trail, our march slowed to a walk.

I'd walked the bush many times at night while on my way home from Leena's. She lived a few miles away from Whispering Cedars on her parents' large dairy farm. Coming home from Pratt and Dolen Secondary School, on my first day, I noticed her reading a book while everyone else horsed around. And on the second day, I struck up a conversation which led to a friendship. I'd visit her on weekends to watch movies, mostly old comedies, sometimes with her and her older brother, Bruce, and his girlfriend, Debbie. These were the memories that surfaced while I walked along a trail on another world.

About halfway to the light, another one appeared. I stopped dead on the trail and raised my hand up to signal the others to stop. The new light joined the other one and they both moved in that high-low circular pattern.

"That's so not them," whispered Tabby. "No way."

"She's right," whispered Colby. "Let's go back to that spot with them unicorns."

Captivated by the lights, I didn't reply. I was unsure of what to do next. Then the pattern changed. The lights revolved low to the ground horizontally, and slowly spiraled up and up to well above head height, then down quickly. And then it hit me. The fire dancers that I watched at a carnival once when I was a kid. I don't know for how long I watched it go on for before Tabby rested a hand on my shoulder, and whispered, "Hey, you still with us?"

"He's all spaced out," whispered Colby.

"Yeah, yeah," I whispered. "I'm fine, just tired, that's all. Let's go."

We set off again, this time side by side, more cautiously, the light display carrying on without interruption. Five minutes later, we arrived at a large patch of dense ferns directly across the riverbank from the lights. We sat catching our breath. We watched the lights move in their hypnotizing pattern. All three of us instinctively crouched lower behind the ferns. I listened intently. I could hear my heart. I could hear their hearts. I could hear the noise of the river, the nature chorus surrounding us. Everything spoke to me right then as rivulets of sweat ran down my forehead, and then I heard a new sound, a humming.

It was a song—that much I was certain of—and it filled the night, rising and lowering, odd yet intriguing and alluring. A second hum joined the first and a moment later they coalesced, one deeper than the other but both performing the same song, like a mournful lullaby expressing profound sadness.

"Told you it ain't the others," whispered Colby triumphantly. "You ever heard Simon sing? He sounds like he got a frog in his throat."

"Maybe they've seen the others," whispered Tabby. "Whoever they are."

Through the plants and trees, I could make out two human figures, small and vague, swinging the lights around.

"We got no idea who they are," I whispered. Then I felt that same warm sensation on my chest. The stone inside the medicine pouch began to heat up. I turned around to scan the forest. At first, I couldn't see anything, but then as my eyes adjusted, I made out another figure: this one a tall shadow in the center of the trail. Colby turned around about to speak. But he stopped. He too fixed on the shadow, the whites of his eyes like full moons.

"Hey, guys, I think they're female," whispered Tabby. She was still watching the light display across the river, unaware that Colby and I were now focused on the quickly-becoming-menacing figure behind us. Without looking, I backhanded her shoulder.

She turned around and whispered, "What?"

Colby pointed at the figure. The three of us watched for what seemed like minutes, waiting to see if it would move or speak. All the while the performance carried on behind us across the river.

I found myself questioning what I was seeing. Had we been so focused on the lights that we missed an abnormally shaped tree trunk? Or maybe it was an animal? We'd only been there for a day, who knew what other strange creatures, mythical creatures even, lived on that world.

Then whatever it was made a loud clicking noise, sending a jolt through my body.

Other figures swiftly emerged from the undergrowth, like angry hornets from a disturbed hive. There were so many that I wasn't able to keep track of all of them at first, but when they finally stopped moving, I counted thirteen in total. This wasn't good, and it was only worsening by the moment.

The first figure, who was broad-shouldered and taller than the rest, came toward us. I'd like to say that I didn't contemplate turning to flee, but I did. But to where? Into the river? Through the forest? Only then to be chased down by whomever they were. As the tall figure closed the distance, my heart quickened and hands trembled. A raw fear grew inside of me, the kind of fear that I'd only experienced a few times in my young life. The figure reached a spot on the trail where the orange moony light reached the ground, and he became a man. He had a large forehead, fierce eyes, and chestnut skin. He looked as though he'd stepped right out of an old black-and-white Indian picture of the kind that I'd seen while perusing books in the library. I guessed him for the leader.

"Give me the gym bag," I said to Tabby, reaching for it. She handed me the bag. I slowly went inside and removed the fruit-and-nut bar.

"What are you doing?" she said.

I peeled back the wrapper and gestured the bar to my mouth, and then giving my friendliest smile, I cautiously handed it to the leader. He sniffed a few times before taking a small bite. His eyes widened and he spit a mouthful at my feet and tossed the bar over his shoulder. He spoke rapidly in a strange language, that there was something oddly familiar about.

"Oh, great move," said Colby. "He royally pissed now."

Two others came up to the leader's side, both carrying spears.

"Put up your hands," I said to Tabby and Colby, raising my hands above my head. Tabby's shot up, but Colby was slow to move so I elbowed him in the ribs.

When I heard a commotion behind me, I turned around. Three very capable-looking Indians held spears, the points inches away from our heads.

"Man, this all bad, bad, bad, like real bad," said Colby from the side of his mouth.

Neither Tabby nor I spoke. My heart beat like a jackhammer in my chest, and sweat began to run into my eyes.

"If they wanted to kill us, they'd of done it already," said Colby.

"How do you know?" said Tabby.

They were talking too loud, and I didn't like it.

"You know 'bout snakes. I know 'bout gangs," said Colby.

A stir went through our ambushers. The spearheads that had been focused on Tabby and me moved to Colby. Three spearheads made of ivory or bone were ready to shish kebob his head.

There was a shout behind me. When I turned to look, a spear point jabbed my left butt cheek. It prodded me forward until I was face to face with the leader. He uttered something in his language. The other Indians surrounded us, moving as swiftly and surely as the tactical team that had arrested Uncle Hanker and me in that highway motel. They forced us to our knees. Strong hands clutched my arms, which were still overhead, twisted them around my back, and began tying them together. Tabby and Colby got the same treatment.

"You all right, Tabby?" I said.

"Hey, man, those so tight my hands gonna fall off," hissed Colby.

"Pretty sure they can't understand you," said Tabby.

"Whatcha saying?" said Colby.

"She's saying they don't speak English," I said.

The Indians tightened their circle around us at this first sign of rebellion, shouting angrily and thrusting their spears toward our faces. And I remembered feeling the same way when the police arrested Uncle Hanker and me. The seventy-two thousand dollars from our bank robberies had been neatly stacked on the dresser.

Uncle Hanker planned to send his sons money for college tuition, and I planned to replace my mother's gravestone with an actual headstone. I didn't know why those thoughts came to me right then, but they did. Maybe because I realized right then and there that I'd never get to fulfill my dream, with the way things were going.

We were helpless. There was nothing we could do but allow things to unfold.

Colby turned to me and gave his defiant look, like he was about to try something.

"Don't fight. Please don't fight," I said. "Not the time or place for it." My eyes and mouth narrowed and I shook my head slightly, hoping to affirm my message. The bonds around my wrist cinched tight.

The leader began to speak hurriedly to the others, as if he was giving orders.

"This isn't good," said Tabby.

"No, it isn't," I said. "Let's go peacefully, but if there's a chance to move then we all need to be ready."

"What about my uncle and Anna and Simon?" said Tabby.

"Man, worry 'bout them later," said Colby.

Before I could reply, we were hauled to our feet. Who knew if there'd be a later?

13

A single file line formed, us in the center, the leader at the head. Then we started toward the river. The lights had ceased moving and were simply there in the forest like whoever was using them had stopped due to the commotion and was waiting now to see what would happen next. Then I saw them. Tabby was right. They were female. Two girls actually. They held poles tipped with baskets in which were bunches of glowing orbs.

Tossing his hands in the air, the leader gesticulated angrily and yelled at the girls. They fled into the forest, their lights fading off after them.

A narrow log spanned the forty feet from bank to bank. The leader began to cross nimbly, the other Indians ahead of me following just as easily. When it came my turn, I hesitated a moment before I stepped on, feeling a slight quiver running the length of the log. I stole a quick glance at the river below, then started across, swaying back and forth a few times like a drunken tightrope walker, minus the pole and adoring fans. My arms would've helped but they were slowly going numb, cinched tightly behind me as they were. And my knee ached something fierce. The others followed across, and it wasn't until I was on the other bank that I looked back to see both Tabby and Colby traversing the last quarter of the log bridge, doing surprisingly well.

The trail widened threefold, and we followed in single file, passing other intersecting trails as we went along. We'd been quietly walking for some time when Tabby whispered my name, and said, "Where do you think they're taking us?"

"They're not packing a lot of gear," I whispered. "Can't be too far from their home."

"We gonna let this happen?" said Colby way too loudly, coming up beside us, so that we were in a tight cluster.

"First chance we get we lose them in the forest," I whispered back.

"These guys look like they're part of the forest," whispered Tabby. She was surely right—they'd give chase if we made a break.

"I ain't gonna let them roast me over a fire. No way, man. I ain't no one's dinner," said Colby. "I want to see sunrise."

Suddenly the leader whirled around and strode back toward us, causing us to disperse like guilty conspirators. He headed straight for Colby and said, "I prefer fish and berries." And then just as quickly as he'd come, he returned to the front of the line.

The three of us looked at one another, the same shocked faces. He'd spoken perfect English, not broken, not accented, not slang. He'd spoken American English like the kind I'd been hearing all my life in malls, in schools, in theatres, in supermarkets. I didn't even attempt trying to talk to Tabby and Colby again. But I could tell from their faces that they were as baffled as me. The alien Indian had spoken impeccable English. Who knew what was next?

Barking dogs and hints of woodsmoke told me that we were approaching a camp or settlement of some type. The sounds and smells increased as we neared. I wasn't sure whether to feel relief or anxiety. In all the movies and stories I'd seen and read in which prisoners were taken to villages by their captors, it always seemed to end up with those prisoners being tortured, maimed, killed, and/ or eaten. And I tried to remember if any ever walked away after, and none came to me in those nerve-racking moments as we got closer and closer to our destination.

Flames appeared through the trees up ahead, rearing up into the night sky. A pack of a dozen or so dogs that looked to be half-wolf, half-husky ran out to greet us. They dashed back and forth on either side of the line, barking, giving throaty growls, sniffing the air like they were unsure what to make of us prisoners.

The trees thinned out and the outline of a village began to form in the dark. There were no cars, no dumpsters, no streetlights, no houses. There were no sidewalks or parking lots. In the clearing, there stood hide-covered tepees and firepits with racks next to them on which hung strips of some type of meat. Men, women, and children walked around all dressed in the same hide outfits as our captors.

As we entered, Indians of all ages emerged from everywhere, children peering from around adults' legs, adults staring with a mixture of wariness and curiosity. I wondered if they'd ever laid eyes on the likes of us before in their village. By the way they were acting, I figured they hadn't.

"Look at that fish. He wasn't lying," said Colby, nodding at a drying rack draped in long fish fillets. He gave his toothy smile that I hadn't seen since before the landslide, since before the game against St. Michael's. I felt slightly eased, as if Colby's smile made everything all right, because the only time he gave toothy was when things were all right. Then I thought how foolish that was. Basing my assessment of our situation on a smile, especially his. How desperately hopeful I was being.

Out of nowhere, a dog nipped my heel, then darted away to run parallel to me at about ten feet out. A mangy looking black-and-white mutt, that could've been a border collie crossed with a wiener dog. It was smaller than all the others, more brazen as well, or so it seemed. Its tongue lolled from the side of its mouth. One eye was missing.

Its tail wagged as if it was playing a game: nipping me and running off. It looked like a homeless dog that you'd find scrounging around a dumpster in an inner-city alley. The kind that you felt sorry for, but would still never take home.

The farther we got into the village, the more Indians appeared. They formed a corridor, like a gauntlet, that we walked along. Two faces stood out as I passed by. Their skin was noticeably a lighter brown than the others, a mocha color. They were girls, identical looking, pretty, with almond eyes.

A mother emerged from a tepee cradling a whimpering baby to her chest. Then a round face appeared in the dark opening of another, and a girl began to call out to her mother. A group of young boys were sitting in a circle around one fire, sharpening sticks with black stones like obsidian that reflected in the firelight. An old Indian with long wavy gray hair was sitting beside them, speaking quietly, moving his hands gracefully through the air as though he was sharing a story. They fixed on us, joining the other onlookers. At the next fire sat ten or so women with long raven hair, weaving strips of bark and talking. They glanced at us briefly before going back to their weaving.

"They living like animals," said Colby. "No bathrooms, no nothing."

"That makes them animals?" said Tabby. "It's like a pre-contact village."

"A pre-*what*?" said Colby.

"A Native American village before Europeans arrived," I said. "Two hundred years ago this was how people lived in North America. It's similar to how your people lived in Africa."

"Man, you talking that mumbo-jumbo like you a big know-it-all, just like Anna," said Colby.

"I think they're taking us there," I said, and nodded to a large rustic-looking longhouse a short distance ahead. It was made from horizontal logs, gray and checked like they'd been exposed to the elements for many years. A dark fur draped half open in the doorway, revealing firelight flickering deep within.

14

When we arrived, the leader stepped aside at the entrance and spoke his language. The other Indians stopped. He spoke more words. Ten of them headed back into the heart of the village, leaving us with the leader and two others who were the complete opposites of each other: one chubby with a round head, and the other skinny with a long nose. The leader gave us the once-over—one by one—not speaking or giving any clues as to what he might be thinking.

Colby hopped from foot to foot, almost dancing. "I got to take a whiz, man," he said. "Bladder gonna blow."

"Not in the longhouse," said the leader. He tossed his chin at his sidekicks, then said, "They'll show you where *we animals* go." He motioned for me and Tabby to enter the longhouse. The skinny Indian grabbed Colby by the arm and tried to lead him around the side.

I went to stop him. "We're not leaving him."

The leader stiffened immediately and stepped in front of me, so we were nose to nose. With this closeness, I realized he was over six feet tall, taller than Colby, and rangy and muscular like a farmer who'd been toiling away on the land his entire life.

The whole thing reminded me of Peter Murray, the bully who'd accosted me on my first night at the youth detention facility in Portland, clenching his fists and ordering me—the new fish—to give up my snack, or he'd pump my eyes shut. I agreed to give it to him, not because I was frightened by his threat or by the fact he was mean-looking and thirty pounds heavier, but because I was dog-tired and thought if we scrapped I'd be good for nothing and end up on the losing end. I went to my room, picked up my apple, dipped it in toilet water, gave it a quick flick and blow, and then walked out. Straight-faced, not a slump in either shoulder, and in front of everyone, I handed him my apple. I slept surprisingly well on my first night in youth detention, all things considered.

"You do not have a choice," said the leader, jarring me out of my memory.

The chubby Indian placed his bone spearhead against my chest and gave it a light poke, then gestured the tip to the doorway, as if saying I better move or else. The leader laid a hand on the spear's shaft without taking his eyes off me and pushed it aside.

"Your friend will come in after he is done," he said.

"You sure about that?" I said, studying his face.

He looked to Colby, then to me. I got the feeling he was being straight.

"It's all right," said Colby. We held each other's eyes for a moment. He gave me a look that said he'd be fine. So I entered the longhouse, Tabby following, unsure of myself, unsure of what we would face.

15

The fires roar high in the twilight and the tang of roasted flesh lingers in the air. The drummers beat their drums and the dancers start to ghost dance. Dejunga is becoming lost in a trance. He is journeying with all the Wendo braves stretching back the generations that had come before him, as if already stalking his prey, his ghost moccasins whispering on the forest floor. The thrill races his heart.

When he opens his eyes, the five other braves that have been selected are standing straight up as he is, bound to wooden posts with strips of skin from those who have sacrificed themselves for the hunt. Night is upon them and Blood Sun has dipped behind the mountain. It will be a good hunt; the daylong ghost ceremony assuring that Dejunga and the braves will be successful in what it is they will set out to do at dawn.

They enjoyed watching the sacrifices to the Creator, enjoyed feasting as he feasted, drinking as he drank. The flesh for their ghost moccasins was peeled from the soles of the feet of those who gave themselves, then sewn and set out on drying racks by the firepit. Each pair made custom for a brave. Not a scrap has been wasted, even the dogs' bellies filled.

The ghost dancers whirl and thrust their arms to the sky. The sounds filling Dejunga's ears are the most sacred sounds, old as the Wendo. As his face is wrapped in ghost skin, he remembers a time when their tribal chieftain, Godacka, rose from the womb of Mother Earth to lead their people against the pale-skin Yankees. They had been encroaching on Wendo territory, slaughtering their buffalo, murdering hunters and children. He remembers the skirmishes, and in the beginning, the Wendo's numerous victories. He remembers the scalps they cut from the heads of their fallen enemies to hang on their belts, and the horses, food, and other trinkets they took from a pale-skin people they did not understand. A people not born to survive in the land the Wendo had called home since the dawn of Mother Earth. Then things had changed.

The Yankees came with more and more men, more and more muskets, and it was in this way they overwhelmed the Wendo as a flooding river overwhelms its banks, slowly rising until it is unstoppable. The Wendo were forced to flee their land when their scouts came with word of the approaching Yankee army, and they were faced with a choice: pack up and strike out into the coldest, fiercest winter storm the elders could remember, or stay and be cut down by the Yankees' muskets and swords.

The storm engulfed them.

They lost over one hundred people in the first two days, three hundred on the second. The remaining two hundred were forced to trudge through the blinding and stinging white, as a wounded deer's instincts force it on, aware the hunter is in pursuit.

Only when the snow had become so deep they could no longer walk did they stop and erect a makeshift camp and huddle together— the old praying, the children weeping—from the frigid cold to await death. Many died.

In the morning, the surviving Wendo emerged from their shelters into a world that had changed somewhere during the night. It was then that the Wendo had been reborn into a new world, the World of Dawn. But they would soon return to the Mother Earth and exact their revenge.

Dejunga feels a presence near him, then a voice croaks, "Bring me the Boy with the Scar." He grins under the ghost skin, and among the Wendo, Dejunga is not known as a man who grins.

16

The air in the longhouse was heavy and sooty, reminding me of charred firewood the morning after a heavy rain. A firepit lay in the center. The flames I'd seen from outside danced and crackled, reaching up toward an opening in the ceiling. Around the fire were large bundles of fur. On the far side, two older Indians were sitting and watching us as we were lead toward them. From what I could tell, there were no other people inside, but the shadows outside the fire's radius were deep enough that if someone wanted to remain hidden they wouldn't have had any difficulty. The older Indians didn't move or speak, while Tabby and I were prodded forward to the inner circle. I felt tiny inside that place in front of those men, almost like a child.

One of the Indians had a broad face and steep forehead, black hair to his shoulders. He sat erect, more so than anyone I'd ever seen, real dignified-like. To the right of him sat an ancient man with a wizened face, long wispy gray hair, so thin he was like a skeleton mummified in wrinkly skin. His eyes were half closed and he rocked back and forth slightly, holding a walking stick in both his hands as if he was supporting his body from falling over.

We stood there silently for what seemed like minutes, Tabby and I under their strong gazes, before a noise behind us drew our attention. The skinny Indian had entered the longhouse with Colby, who looked around, a bit startled, trying to take everything in. They took up beside Tabby.

"You found all three," said the Indian with the broad face. He nodded, pleased.

"We found them at the crossing, spying on your daughters," said the leader.

"We ain't spying on nobody," said Colby firmly, like he did when he thought he was being falsely accused.

"We saw lights and thought it was our friends," I said.

"My uncle broke his leg," said Tabby worriedly. "He needs help."

The older Indian with the broad face began speaking calmly in his language to the ancient Indian. Before he even finished, the leader who'd brought us in reached behind his back and came out with a steel bowie knife, which glinted in the firelight. I backed up and either Colby or Tabby let out a sharp breath. We jostled about a moment, then settled into a huddle, our backs tight against one another. My body tensed, readying to move if he lifted the blade to attack.

The leader went toward Colby, his face a stony mask, void of any sign of intention. Colby back-pedaled, tripped, and thudded butt first on the longhouse floor. The way he brandished the knife, I got the feeling he knew how to use it, the way Vince used one back at Whispering Cedars. I stepped in between them. "You said we'd see sunrise, now you're going to kill us? You're a bald-faced liar," I yelled.

He stopped abruptly, his eyes widening for a split second before turning to slits, then he turned to the Indian with the broad face like he was unsure of what he should do next. At that point, my heartbeat was like the running of the bulls in my chest, drowning out the crackle of the flames. Then ancient Indian chuckled, a resounding chuckle that I would've never guessed possible from such an old and frail-looking man.

Broad face gestured a hand at the ancient man. "Your courage makes Glixtan laugh. Not in twenty years have I heard him laugh in such a way . . . Glooscap means no harm. He will cut the bonds at your wrists."

I reached down and grasped Colby's hand and helped him to his feet. Colby hesitated a moment, then he turned around and gave Glooscap his back and lifted his bound hands up as far as he could. With a flick of the blade, the bonds fell away to the longhouse floor. Colby brought his hands in front of him and rubbed his wrists. I gave Glooscap my back and I felt the lick of cold steel against my flesh before my bonds fell to the floor.

The last time my wrists had felt that way was during my sentencing hearing in Seattle, after one of the hype-case sheriffs clicked my handcuffs too tight, right before he told me that his twenty-year-old niece had been working at one of the banks we'd robbed. Later that afternoon, while standing behind the polished oak table beside my public defender, I listened to Judge Henry's two options: youth detention for a year followed by a year in the state prison, or two years at a farm for troubled youth, Halton House. I wasn't stupid. I chose Halton House. When that same sheriff removed the cuffs, he scoffed and said I deserved a year in the Big House, with the big boys. Said it would only be a matter of time before I was Bubba's girlfriend.

After Glooscap cut Tabby free, we stood shoulder to shoulder, facing the two men that we'd been brought to see. Glooscap, Skinny, and Chubby stayed off to the side, all quiet-like, all respectful as if they'd been through this before and knew the protocol to be followed.

"My name is Poowasan," said the Indian with the broad face. "I am chief of the Sawnay people. Your bodies and spirits are weary. Rest them now and know you are safe. You are guests and will be treated with customs stretching back to when the raven gave life to the sun."

"What about our friends?" I said, looking from Poowasan to Glixtan. "We need to find them." It wasn't that I didn't believe him, but the fact that we had no idea whether or not the others were alive or dead was weighing on me so heavily that if I didn't have an answer soon, I might be crushed to dust. That still might happen if the answer wasn't the one I was hoping for.

Poowasan spoke in Sawnay to Glooscap, who exited the longhouse with Chubby and Skinny, leaving us alone with the two older men. I figured it ripe time for us to escape, and possibilities began to race through my mind. Glixtan looked directly into my eyes and held me locked there for a moment, giving a toothless smile, like he'd sensed something, like he'd sensed what I'd been thinking. My face grew warm, and I looked down at my toes.

"How did we get here?" said Tabby.

Raising his stick high above his head, Glixtan pointed at the opening above the firepit and spun the stick three-sixty. Then a loud noise behind us drew our attention. The three of us turned around. Glooscap had entered the longhouse, and coming in behind him, limping on crutches, was Conroy, followed by Anna and Simon.

17

We rushed toward them as they rushed toward us, and met them in the middle of the longhouse floor. Glooscap tried to step in between the reunion, but when Poowasan hollered in Sawnay, he backed off. We began hugging one another excitedly, the swirling tempest of worry we'd been feeling for hours quickly subsiding. We were so caught up in our jubilation at learning the others were alive—and hadn't been snatched and devoured by giant birds, or lost somewhere in that vast prehistoric forest—that we carried on for minutes.

Conroy looked able on crutches, his face no longer pale and tense, but full of color and warmth. Anna and Simon looked well too, no longer covered in mud, lost in an air of shell shock. They all seemed revitalized. Although it had only been several hours, it seemed like they'd had an opportunity to rest and recuperate from the landslide as well as the shock of awakening to find out they were on another world, far, far away from everything they'd ever known, everything they'd ever cherished.

"Can't *believe* you guys are here," said Simon.

"We had no idea what happened to you," I said.

"These monster birds dove and started snatching deer," said Tabby, her hands imitating wings.

"I know—we saw them right before the Sawnay took us into the forest," said Anna.

"Crazy, crazy place, man. The stuff we seen," said Colby. "Tell them 'bout the unicorns. Just like in the stories."

"Unicorns? Like real unicorns?" said Anna.

"Yeah, all white. Big horn coming out the head," said Colby excitedly.

"Cool," said Simon.

"The important thing is we're all together and safe," said Conroy, hugging his nieces together. "We'll figure things out tomorrow—it's so good to see you three. We didn't want to leave, but Glooscap promised us he'd go back for you as soon as we were safe."

"Didn't seem so friendly when he first came up on us," said Colby, glaring at Glooscap.

"We followed the trail along the river," I said. "Then Glooscap found us."

"I take it Anna's phone didn't get any reception?" said Conroy.

Before the last words left his mouth, I knew that Anna's iPhone was no longer in my pocket. I couldn't recall how long it had been since I'd last checked for it. With all the action, excitement, and worry, I'd totally forgotten that I'd been carrying it in my pocket. Maybe I'd lost it on the bluff when I leapt into the trees or as I dropped through the boughs, or maybe as we hustled down the mountain. I had no idea. Then I remembered the text messages, and couldn't help but glance at Anna's stomach, only to not find any obvious bulge in the shadows.

"No, there wasn't—I think I lost it on the mountain," I said guiltily.

Anna waved her hand as though it was no big deal. "I sort of needed an excuse to buy a new one anyhow."

"I wouldn't hold your breath," said Simon. "I don't see there being any Best Buys around here."

"At least we ain't gonna die listening to her crappy retro," said Colby, and he fist-bumped Simon.

"Come sit by the fire," said Poowasan calmly.

We were still huddled in a small circle, focused on one another, closed off from everything that wasn't us, like we were holding on to that moment to make sure it was real, like some comforting dream that we didn't want to wake up from.

"Let's have a seat," said Conroy, nodding toward the fire. Together we headed over to the firepit where we began to sit down on those hide cushions. Simon and I took a hold of Conroy's arms and lowered him down so that his legs were kicked out in front of him, the crutches at his side. They were made from tree branches, the actual crutch sections were Ys, wrapped in hide. Anna sat down on his right, Tabby on his left. Simon, Colby, and then me only an arm's length from Glixtan.

Glooscap told us the names of the other two Indians when they sat down on the remaining two cushions: Chubby was actually Broden, and Skinny was Cawop. I got the feeling the three of them were tight. We formed an unbroken human ring around the firepit, and with this, the circle seemed smaller, more intimate. Having all the seats filled somehow brought us all closer together under the roof of that longhouse, and I no longer felt tiny. The tension eased for the first time since our short-lived respite at the river, but even that was different. Here, there was no possibility of wild animals—either earthly or alien—attacking us. There was no chance of us being caught out in the cold or foul weather. We were warm, safe. All together.

"Thank you for bringing us here, Poowasan," said Conroy. "You did as you said, and I'm grateful for your hospitality and the medical attention you and your people have given us." I hadn't noticed at first, but Conroy's leg had been re-splinted. By the firelight I could see a bandage of some type covering the wound, and his eye was no longer as red as it had been. And Anna's eye. It wasn't swollen shut anymore.

Glixtan stood. Without his walking stick, he hobbled over to Simon. He shut his eyes and spoke in Sawnay, reaching for a pouch on his hip. Praying quietly, he opened the pouch. He placed his finger inside, then touched it to Simon's forehead and made little circular motions, leaving an ochre-colored powder on his skin. Simon's eyes closed as he sat there unmoving.

When Glixtan finished, he went to Colby and performed the same treatment. Then he came to me. He stared into my eyes before placing his finger against my skin. The powder smelled like rich soil. A tingling sensation began to spread across my forehead, stronger with every circle, slowly washing down my neck and into my chest and back, even out to my arms and down my legs. All the muscles in my body twitched and tingled, the ache in my knee dissipated. It was one of the strangest experiences that I'd ever had. I don't know how long it went on for, but when I opened my eyes, Glixtan had already sat back down on his cushion to the right of me. He spoke in Sawnay, dumping powder from his pouch into his hand. Then he tossed it into the fire. Flames crackled and shot to life, launching sparks up through the opening in the ceiling, as if a ferocious gust of wind had blown through the door. The blast of heat caused us newcomers to lean back from the fire, and caused the Sawnay to erupt in good-natured laughter.

Poowasan spoke to Glooscap, who then stood up and left the longhouse. I remained silent—deep in thought—my mind replaying the day's events: the landslide; Carol's death; the hike to the bluff; the attack of the giant birds; discovering Conroy and the girls missing; the trek into the forest; the river with its flying fish and the encounter with the unicorns; the hypnotic light show; and finally our capture.

To me it felt like it had all happened days ago, when in reality it'd been merely hours. And then those events changed to questions: Where were we? Who really were these people? What had happened to us? And what would happen tomorrow, and the day after, and the day after that? Or was this entire thing all a dream? Would I awake in a few minutes back at Halton House—on Earth—Simon in the bed next to me, mumbling in his sleep like he always did in the early morning? Or would I awake back in my bed at Whispering Cedars, the smell of bacon and eggs wafting in through the crack of my door? There'd be country music playing on the radio in the kitchen, my mother humming along as she prepared breakfast just the way we liked it—crispy bacon, golden hash browns, and sunny-side-up eggs. Was I in the midst of the longest dream I'd ever had? Or maybe a coma? Had I been dreaming for days or weeks or maybe even months? I tried to remember if I'd crashed a dirt bike, spilled from a horse, or been in a car accident. Was I still trapped in the Halton House van unconscious? Was I dead?

There was a draft of air and the flames wavered. A long line of Sawnay men and women began to enter, some carrying baskets woven out of bark and others bloated skins like wineskins. Some had bundles of furs and other articles with them. There had to have been around twenty people of all ages file into the longhouse before the fur dropped again, leaving the inside feeling much smaller, not uncomfortable smaller, but closer and cosier. The newcomers started to sit down in an outer circle around us, setting down the items that they'd brought in with them.

One middle-aged, round-faced woman, smiling warmly, set two baskets down in front of us. She gestured her hand to her mouth, like she was eating from it. Inside one basket there was a medley of berries, and in the other were long strips of dried meat the length of my hand.

A girl with a long braid, really pretty, handed Conroy one of the skins. He took it from her, swished it side to side, pulled the plug from the nipple and sniffed the contents. Beaming, she urged, with nods and hand gestures, for Conroy to drink up. He lifted the nipple to his lips, tilted the skin back, and took a long drink. The woman and girl cooed with delight. And it was then I noticed how much they resembled each other, so much so I thought they might've been sisters, or maybe mother and daughter.

My stomach growled loudly. Simon turned and whispered: "Think it's safe?"

"My stomach says *yes*," I whispered back.

"Good enough for me," said Colby, and he reached into the basket for a handful of berries, which he started wolfing down.

Simon and Conroy went straight for the strips of meat and began to scarf away. I waited until Anna and Tabby had both taken some berries, before I scooped a handful. They exploded in my mouth— sweet, succulent, refreshing. I devoured handful after handful, placating my growling stomach. Anna passed me the skin, the plug dangling by a strip of hide. I washed down the berries with two long gulps of a juice-like liquid that tasted and smelled somewhat like dandelions. After a few swigs, I passed it to Simon. Then it struck me—I'd been so caught up stuffing my face that I'd forgotten about our hosts. I glanced around the longhouse at the round dusky faces glowing in the firelight. All the Sawnay were staring at us. I stopped and wiped juice from my chin, focused on Poowasan, wondering if we'd been disrespectful without even knowing it.

Poowasan spoke loudly: "The food was brought for all of us."

Conroy and the others paused in the middle of what they were doing and looked up. A long, awkward silence followed, longer and more awkward than most. Then Poowasan slapped his thighs merrily, roaring with laughter, and all the other Sawnay joined in. Conroy started laughing. Then the rest of us burst out, until everyone in the longhouse was in an uproar of laughter that carried on and on and on. Despite all that had happened, we were there together, sharing pure human laughter, the deep-down kind. It was unforced, totally natural. The kind that made your sides hurt. The kind you never wanted to stop for nothing. The kind I hadn't experienced since Whispering Cedars. And I didn't want it to end. I wanted it to go on and on until I couldn't laugh any longer, and it did. It went on for minutes before dying down. For the first time, in a long time, I was completely laughed out.

When it finally subsided, the longhouse was calmer, as though everyone needed time to recover, leaving the mood lighter, more open and friendlier. That was how good it was. Even Glooscap's fierce eyes had changed to something much softer. He no longer looked like he was spoiling for a fight, like he was carrying around an anger that needed to be purged. One of the newcomers then produced a large shell with smoldering, aromatic contents. He carried a feather and brushed everyone down with the cedary smoke.

"Smudge," said Simon, and nodded when it came to my turn. "To clean your spirit."

Poowasan spoke in Sawnay to the newcomers. There was movement in the shadows. Some of them began to don heavy furs and colorful masks and pick up the other items that they'd brought in, as if they were actors preparing for a show.

One Sawnay man suddenly sprang to his feet and entered the innermost circle, wearing a mask of white, red, black, and yellow on which had been painted friendly eyes and a mouth. In his hand, he carried a large hoop, six feet across, made from thin braided branches that had been intertwined. He began to circle the fire with a side step, waving the hoop back and forth above his head, chanting a song. A man and woman got up and joined in behind the hoop dancer, both young and fur-caped.

They all danced—moving in a wild, primitive way, strangely hypnotizing—raising first their arms and then their knees, bouncing on the balls of their feet. As they circled the fire, the chanting—high and upbeat—grew louder. The other Sawnay began to join in until the entire longhouse resonated with song.

Poowasan spoke loudly to be heard over everyone: "The Sawnay lived for fifty generations on Mother Earth. We lived in harmony with the Grass People, the Tree People, the Animals, the Rock People, and Mother Earth. We cared for her children, and her children grew strong and learned to look deep within themselves for answers to the greatest mysteries, the mysteries that make us who we are."

The chanting lowered until it was barely audible above the lick and crackle of the flames, remaining that way until Poowasan continued speaking, at which time the chanting grew louder again: "The grandfathers spoke to our shamans through dreams, dreams that foretold the coming storm of sickness and death, brought by people from across the Great Water who would come in winged ships."

Two more men entered the innermost circle, holding triangle frames above their heads with hides tightly stretched across them like sails.

Poowasan continued: "We knew many people would die of sickness. We knew we would never see our children or their children grow. We knew we would be stripped from our land as the winter strips the trees of their leaves. Our people made the choice to leave Mother Earth and return to the origin of all life—World of Dawn."

The hoop dancer who was leading the others stopped circling the fire and rested the bottom of the hoop on the ground. The young man and woman stopped near the hoop. When the sailing ships got close, they bounded through the hoop and dashed from the circle into the shadows. Before the ships could pursue them, the hoop dancer lifted the hoop and whirled it around overhead. Then he followed the others into the shadows.

The Sawnay erupted triumphantly in yips and shouts while the two sailing ships circled around the fire aimlessly. Another man and woman entered the circle, wearing masks of black and white on which had been painted frowning eyes and mouths. A different chanting began, a different song, low and deep, sad and mournful.

The sailing ships caught up to the man and woman, and they all mingled in a cluster.

"Other people," said Poowasan, "did not listen to the warnings from the grandfathers. Death came in the form of gifts. Their way of life became the way of fear, the way of hate and war, the way of a white-skinned people from across the Great Water."

The remaining dancers circled slowly one more time, and then rejoined the others in the outer ring. The chanting slowly faded until the fire was the only sound left.

The Sawnay had left Earth through some kind of portal that brought them here, to this world—World of Dawn—where we'd ended up somehow. But unlike the Sawnay, we'd come unintentionally. Had my companions understood the performance, the story, the message it conveyed, what it meant for us?

Poowasan's glowing face looked much older in the dying amber firelight, as if what he'd shared had somehow aged him.

"How do we get home?" I said.

Poowasan didn't answer my question, nor did he answer the dozen other questions that followed from the others. He simply and calmly said that the night was not meant for such talk. It was meant for the Sawnay to welcome their guests. The fire was fed with logs. The flames roared to life. More Sawnay entered the longhouse, bringing with them berries and dried fish and meat, which was passed around and shared with everyone. Everyone ate from the same baskets, drank from the same skins; all the while people gave life to song with voices, rattles, and hand drums.

Once in a while, a Sawnay would enter the inner circle and dance and sing solo. At one point, one of the young Sawnay women pointed at Anna's Gucci purse. Anna passed it around. They examined it with sniffs and squeezes. One young man even bit the strap a few times, and then gave a nod of approval. She had to say the word *Gucci* a dozen times until everyone could repeat it. Oddly, the Sawnay men took the most liking to the purse, with its Gucci label done in rhinestones, especially Cawop who seemed entranced by the way it glimmered in the firelight.

Much later in the night, after it quieted down and the flames shrank, Glooscap shared the story of how they'd found Conroy and the girls. Then he went on to share how they'd found us three at the river, and how he'd heard Colby's fear about being eaten, and then how—in English—he told Colby that he preferred fish and berries. Everyone laughed, and, yes, even Colby.

By the time people began to filter out of the longhouse, well into the night, my eyes were heavy and sore, my body stiffer than if I'd spent a weekend on horseback counting cattle up in Montana's high country. My thoughts slipped away and vanished before I could hold onto any of them, dog-tired as I was.

Tabby and Anna were curled up on either side of their uncle. Simon and Colby had already laid down and wrapped themselves in heavy black furs that had been brought in for us by the Sawnay. Everyone felt safe, secure, and comfortable in the sanctuary of the longhouse, it seemed.

Poowasan stood for the first time since our arrival and rounded the dying fire, coming toward me.

"Thank you," I said, feeling like I should say something. "We'd be lost if Glooscap hadn't found us."

Smiling warmly, Poowasan said, "How can you be lost, Tanner, when you know where you are?" With that, he stepped around Colby and Simon and left the longhouse without a whisper of sound, not even when he went through the door.

I got up and lay down on one of the furs behind me and stretched out. I covered myself up, shutting my eyes, feeling the warmth radiating from the red-hot coals. It was just like those nights out on the Montana range, when the world seemed so open and free.

Then I was asleep.

18

It is a dank, dark place. I drift along a narrow corridor made of ancient blocks, large and moldy. Putrid liquid runs along the ground in narrow channels on either side. It feels like I am swimming or floating in the air, only without kicks or strokes, like a force is pulling me forward.

As I travel farther along, I pass other dark corridors branching off in either direction, some slope up, others slope down. My body accelerates to a breathtaking speed, causing my heart to flutter. I reach a junction where I slow down and without a thought I turn left, before speeding toward a place I know that I do not want to go.

I travel at that breathtaking speed again and I try to will the force to turn me around. Nothing happens. Then in front of me appears a wooden door, scarred as if someone had tried to hack through it with an axe. I get so close so swiftly that I think I will collide with it, but then abruptly stop a foot away and just hover there.

It takes me a sec to calm my heart and catch my breath. At the bottom of the door, there is a gap of an inch. A draft of air is sucking through it, sounding like a person gasping. I slowly reach out my left hand and brush my fingertips over the door's wooden grain, then over the rusty iron of the keyhole plate. The keyhole is large enough for my finger to fit into. Then I hear a groan on the other side.

I lean forward and carefully put my eye to the keyhole. There is only darkness at first, then suddenly a bloodshot eye appears. I jerk back, my heart stampeding in my chest. A violent strike hits the door, reverberating down the corridor like thunder across the open plain.

It happens again, again, and again, as if whoever is on the other side is trying to break through—will break through. Then the force seizes hold of me and drags me backward.

I am unable to see behind me, and I feel sick, like motion sickness, disoriented. In an attempt to slow myself, I stretch out my arms until my fingertips rake along the stone blocks.

They tear on the stone as I scream out in pain.

19

"Tanner, Tanner, the birds sing," said a voice. It took me a sec to realize I was no longer asleep and dreaming. I rolled onto my back, wiping sleep from my eyes, trying desperately to hold my dream together and search for meaning. But it was no use. It fragmented and flitted from my mind. Gone in seconds. Glooscap was knelt over me, a stick in his hand as though he was preparing to prod me awake.

I tossed back the fur that had been keeping me warm and got to my feet. The smoldering coals were dark. Conroy and the others still slept under their furs. Simon mumbled like he usually did early in the morning.

Glooscap pointed the stick at the longhouse entrance. "We must go. They wait for us." Too tired still to ask who "they" were, I simply followed him.

We left the darkness of the longhouse into a pre-sunrise lavender morning, warm and heavy with moisture. Those three-ringed planets were overhead, bright and clear. Same position. Stars flickered stubbornly against the coming day. Swiftly, we cut through the village, Glooscap leading the way, wending around dew-glistening tepees and firepits from which traces of smoke spiraled into the air. The odd-looking, one-eyed dog that had nipped my heel the night before appeared. It started to tail me, keeping about twenty feet back, stopping every time I turned around to look, one good eye fixed on me, goofy tongue dangling from its mouth.

A few minutes later, we entered the forest on a narrow, well-worn trail, the early morning fog so thick I could only make out ten feet or so ahead of me. I could taste the moisture.

The forest had not lost its majestic quality that had awed and frightened me the day before. It felt like even more of a magical place as we went deeper. Strange, colorful birds fluttered overhead, chirruping and twittering. Unseen creatures scurried through the dense undergrowth on either side of the trail. At first I felt some apprehension, but Glooscap never stopped or looked back. He carried on as if it was all natural. So I told myself that if there was something I needed to be aware of, he would tell me. After all, it was his backyard. And he seemed to be a capable woodsman, not to mention the Sawnay had been there for hundreds of years.

Within a minute on the trail, my cobwebs cleared. The forest fog began to dissipate. Glooscap didn't speak, so I kept quiet and followed along five feet or so behind him, waiting to arrive at our destination so I could find out who "they" were. Glooscap moved quickly, silently, and effortlessly like a true creature of the forest. I found myself having to push to keep up, sweat running down my brow.

When we arrived at the riverbank, I finally learned the answer to who "they" were. Poowasan and Glixtan stood staring down at the river. Neither of them looked at us as we approached, not even when we took up beside them. And then I saw what they were focused on. Fish—hundreds of dead fish—were floating belly up. The same kind from the night before. An acrid smell wafted in the air, causing my nose to itch, leaving a chemical taste in the back of my throat. I could hardly believe this was the same river from which we'd drunk and washed from. A river that had been teeming with vibrant life, but was now teeming with foul death.

"Cootamain is the lifeblood of our people," said Poowasan. "It is sick. It dies a little more each season. More days of dead finned ones and four-legged ones and winged ones happen every year. They use the river for life as my people do." Then he looked up to those three planets, only the two highest visible above the treetops. "All this makes the Three Brothers sad."

"We drank from it last night before Glooscap found us," I said, my voice distant.

"If you drink from it now, you will be sick by the time the sun reaches its highest," said Poowasan.

"And dead by nightfall," added Glooscap.

Poowasan sighed like the thought of it pained him greatly.

As I was pondering their words, a white carcass floated by us like a piece of driftwood, its ribs jutted grotesquely against its hide. The head was just below the surface, and on it was a spiraling horn.

I was certain it was the unicorn colt we'd seen the night before that had headed upriver with its mother. And I thought how those two mythical creatures had seemed to greet us at the riverbank, helping to put our minds at ease. A pang of sadness went off deep in my being, which quickly changed to something else. My fists clenched without any thought from me. The longer I watched the colt float down the river, the tighter the clench got until my nails bit into my palms.

"What's making it sick?" I said, turning to Poowasan. "Why's this happening?"

"We do not know. It began eight seasons ago. Two Sawnay parties have journeyed north searching for answers. They have not returned," he said solemnly, and then tilted back his head. A large crow or raven soared over the river, cawing angrily. "They now walk in the Spirit World."

"Our bravest men," said Glooscap.

"Spirit World?" I said.

"Dead," said Glooscap, his voice less than a whisper, the quietest I'd heard him speak thus far.

"How do you know they're dead?" I said. "Maybe they're still searching."

"They visit Glixtan in his dreams," said Poowasan.

Everyone was silent for a moment, watching the long mass of fish floating down the river.

"This reminds me of pictures I've seen of Alberta's oil sands," I said.

"Alberta in the country of Canada?" said Poowasan.

"Yeah, that's right," I said. "It's a place where the land and rivers are being poisoned because of man's greed. Wait—how do you know about Alberta if you came before Europeans arrived?"

"A friend of the Sawnay taught us the borders of North America," said Poowasan.

"There are *more* people here from Earth?" I said, barely containing my surprise.

Before he could answer, Glixtan turned away from the river to gaze north and spoke for the first time. "A wound festers in the mountains. The wound must be healed or the death will continue until we are forced to leave this land—all living things are forced to leave. A land we have called home for five hundred years."

"I wish I could help. I mean . . . I wish we could help," I said. "But Conroy can't walk without crutches—and we're only young, and we're not from here." I felt younger than I actually was, saying it like that. I felt helpless and frustrated—seeing all that death and knowing I couldn't possibly do anything to help. I didn't have it in me. We had our own things to worry about, our own life and death problems. "Do you know how we can get home?"

There was a moment of silence before Poowasan spoke. "A friend of the Sawnay lives two days north in the Black Swamp. We speak English because of him, we know our choice to leave Mother Earth was right because of him."

"Is this the friend who told you about the borders of North America?" I said.

"We shared the way of this world with him, and he shared with us many things about Mother Earth, about the way people walk on their journeys now. He searches for answers that we do not care to know. He will help you if he can. His name is Ambrose. Another party of Sawnay heads north to search for the cause of the sickness. They will take you with them, so you can speak to him."

I thought about Poowasan's offer quickly, trying to figure out what it would mean if I accepted. "What about Conroy?" I said. "He can barely walk."

"Glooscap will take you. The others can stay as guests of the Sawnay."

"I'll have to talk to them," I said.

"Then you will decide," said Poowasan. With that, he and Glixtan both nodded, satisfied. They started off down the trail as if there was no more to discuss. Glooscap stood waiting for me.

"You go ahead. I'll follow the trail back," I said, looking upriver toward the reddish sun peeping over the treetops. I hooded my eyes with a hand, listening to him walk off. As far as I could see, dead fish floated on the river, like some apocalyptic biblical event was taking place. I'd never seen death on that scale before.

A sudden urge to flee the riverbank gripped me, its smell of toxin, of death. I wanted to get as far away as I possibly could—pronto—far away from that sick water that would carry the unicorn colt off the colossal waterfall and on and on until its carcass lodged against rocks miles downriver. Flies would lay their eggs, eggs would hatch into maggots, maggots would eat his flesh, and finally after all that degradation, his bones would sink to the river bottom like those bones on the bottoms of aquariums, lost in the pebbles. The colt had been far too young to die.

The sun's rays reflected on the surface of the river like a long, writhing orange snake, not quite reaching me yet, but getting closer as the sun continued to rise above the treetops.

Seeing it all was another heavy stone for me to carry in my already hefty backpack. Shaking my head and sighing, I thought how I should be at Halton House reading L'Amour or McCarthy under the shade cast by the old oaks in the backyard. Or how I should be watching Hena and her newborn colt—alive and well—trot around the field, or even cleaning out the chicken coop as the hens and roosters strutted around the yard, pecking up insects and gobbling raucously. I definitely shouldn't have been there seeing all that. And why me? Why had Poowasan not shown this to the others? Why not Conroy? He was the adult, the man of the group. Not me. I was only seventeen, pretty much still a kid, not even old enough to buy beer or cigarettes, barely old enough to drive. A kid who—with his uncle— had robbed banks and terrified people. We'd made it so they cringed when they heard loud noises like shouts or doors slam, made it so they had nightmares every night to awake with their hearts trying to pound out of their chests. They shook and sweated because of their frayed nerves every morning as they headed to work, wondering if it would be the day that someone tried to rob their bank again. I'd heard it all in court from the ones who'd been brave enough to stand up and read their victim impact statements. I'd stolen their sense of safety. I made it so they didn't trust people anymore, so they doubted themselves. That was a little of what I'd done. For a brief period of my young life, I became something I despised. And I hated myself for it, and I didn't know that I would ever stop.

Suddenly, a face appeared in the dense undergrowth beside me. It startled me, not because it was a scary face, but because I hadn't expected to see one there. It seemed to be hovering. Then another face popped up beside the first one. That was when I recognized them, the mocha-skinned twins from the night before who I'd seen as Glooscap led us through the village. I don't know how, but I knew right then they were also the performers, with those lights at the river—the girls Glooscap said were Poowasan's daughters.

"Are you going to speak?" said the one who'd appeared first.

It was like the wires from my brain to my mouth were malfunctioning.

"I think we scared him," she said.

"Startled, not scared," I said. "Why were you singing and waving those lights last night?"

The talkative one emerged from the undergrowth. Her black hair was in two long braids, one on either side of her shoulders. She was dressed like all the other Sawnay in hide shirt and pants. She gave me the once-over with her almond eyes, and then both of them fixed on me. They were silent and didn't seem interested in answering my question whatsoever, just staring at me as if I was some kind of oddity, which I guess I was to them. Then her sister, the quiet one, pushed aside the undergrowth and stepped out beside her.

Their silence started to weird me out. "Well?" I said, with more irritation than I'd planned.

"A mourning ceremony for our father," said the talkative one. "He journeyed north in search of answers and has not yet returned. My name is Chana. My sister is Maroona."

The quiet one, Maroona, turned to look at the dead fish, her lips turning upside down in a frown. She shut her eyes tightly like the sight hurt tremendously. She began humming a song.

Chana spoke, "They say our father no longer walks this world, when we are not around them. Glixtan says his spirit will return to our people." She rested a hand on her sister's shoulder and faced the river. "Maroona prays for the dead creatures."

"Hey, I thought Poowasana is your father?"

"He has taken us into his family as daughters."

Maroona continued her prayer, making me feel awkward. So I did the only thing I could think of doing. I joined in the vigil.

Five minutes later, she finished her prayer. Half the sun shone over the treetops, blazing brightly and warm on my face, the orange writhing reflection on the river now passing me.

"Maroona has not spoken since our father left. They do not think she will speak until our father's spirit returns."

"What if it never returns?" I said.

"It will return," she said with a conviction that made me believe she honestly felt it would. She rubbed her sister's back. "He visits us in our dreams and tells us he will return."

Fragments of my dream flitted through my mind—the weightlessness, the zooming along the corridor, the scarred wooden door, and that eye looking back at me through the keyhole. Then they vanished before I could piece them together into a coherent episode. A spell of dizziness struck me. Stars danced across my vision. I staggered backward, briefly losing my equilibrium.

Chana reached her small hand toward me, a gold ring on her finger glinting in the sun.

"Are you well, Tanner?" she said, concern in her voice.

Backing away, I blinked my eyes a few times, taking a deep breath to get some oxygen to my brain. "I'm fine," I said, wiping a cold sweat from my brow. "How do you know my name?"

She gave a patient smile like what I'd asked was a foolish question. She pointed at her ears. "That is why the Creator gave us these, to hear names." Then she brushed her fingers along her cheek, and said, with the innocence of a child, "What happened to your face?"

I touched the scar that ran across my cheek. No one had asked me that question in a long time. "I had an accident when I was a kid."

She stared at me for a moment, then said, "I must go." She said a few words to Maroona before they both turned and headed off on the trail toward the village.

"You're leaving?" I said, feeling we hadn't finished yet.

Chana paused to look back, letting Maroona carry on. "It is forbidden for anyone to be at the river while the poison runs." Then she followed her sister.

I watched them go, thinking how peculiar they were: identical looking, but very different personalities, opposites really, like black and white, north and south. They rounded a bend on the trail and were lost to sight. They were Sawnay, but different in some way that I couldn't quite put my finger on. It wasn't just their lighter skin, but also the way they acted, as if they walked to the beat of their own drum, as if their life there—the Sawnay's rules and customs—didn't define how they chose to act. They were rule breakers, free spirits. They'd been out last night by themselves, at the river this morning while the poison ran. I figured they'd been hiding in the undergrowth the entire time we'd been speaking, and heard every word that was said.

I wondered if I'd ever see them again. After deciding I wouldn't, I stole a final glance at the floating death still passing by, no end in sight, a true trail of carnage. As I started back to the village, I noticed my fingertips were raw and scratched.

20

Dejunga leads his eight braves down the mountain path toward the Valley of No Name, silent and swift as wolves stalking their prey. Ragaroo had selected them because of their loyalty, their cruelty. They will not disappoint. When it comes to hunting men or animals, their prowess is unmatched.

Dejunga sees something on the path. He kneels down and picks up a strange shine box the size of his hand. He turns it, sniffing it once, then again. A face appears. A Yankee girl, her eyes covered by a black mask. He stares at her white skin, at her pink lips for a moment. He has never seen such a shine box before. But the Wendo have come across many strange things since they left Mother Earth—large metal birds on the ground with their bellies split open, strangely dressed dead inside; men dressed in colorful outfits riding loud horses with wheels instead of legs, and huge beasts that rumbled across the land, black smoke billowing from their backsides. Yes, many strange things.

Deciding to take the shine box with him, he opens one of his hip pouches and puts it inside. After they catch the Yankees and return to their village, he will give the shine box to Ragaroo as a gift and earn his favor. The Creator will tell Ragaroo what it is for.

The Boy with the Scar is the only one who matters. One Who Sees All wants him, and Dejunga will make sure he gets what he wants. But he and his braves will be honored if they return with more Yankee prisoners, and the ceremony will go on for days as the Wendo feast on their spirits, on their flesh.

Dejunga lifts a shriveled head from where it is tied to his hip. The Yankee girl on the shine box is a head he would like to have on his belt, to put with all the other totems he wears on his many hunts and ghost journeys. There is room for one more.

As they descend into the valley, the braves do not speak. They rarely do when hunting. At the foot of the slope, the ground is covered in fresh earth as though it rained from the sky recently. Dejunga smells a familiar scent in the air. He follows it to a rock, and on it he spots a red stain. He kneels down. He licks his finger and rubs the blood. He tastes it. He knows it well. Human blood.

Hulaka approaches him, pointing toward the Skytree Forest. "Two parties. One large Sawnay party, followed by a smaller one of Yankees."

Dejunga gazes toward the skytrees. He hates Sawnay territory, where the spirits of their ancestors are strong among the trees and where he is reminded of the anger that he feels for those who despise the Wendo, those who believe themselves higher in the Creator's eyes than the Wendo.

The Sawnay and Wendo were allies at one time, hunting the same forests, fishing the same rivers. The Sawnay had lived on World of Dawn for many generations and taught the ways of it to the Wendo. But then things changed when the Creator began speaking differently to the Wendo's shaman, Ragaroo. The Creator told him that Chief Godacka had lost his belief, and would never lead the Wendo back to Mother Earth to reclaim their land and take revenge upon the Yankees. So, Godacka was sacrificed, feasted upon during a ghost ceremony to appease the Creator, so the Wendo would be his children again.

Then the other sacrifices began, then the feasting, and then more feasting. And the friendship between the Wendo and Sawnay ended. The way of the Wendo became a different way.

Hulaka waits for him to speak, the Three Brothers shining above him in the Blood Dawn.

"We go where they go, until they go no farther," says Dejunga.

With his finger, he wipes the blood one last time, sucks it clean, then stands up. He steps down from the rock and wades through the long grass toward the skytrees, his eight braves trailing behind, silently, ghostly.

There is a fluttering of wings. A small blackbird is flying toward Dejunga. He puts out his hand and the blackbird lands on his finger. It coos as he lifts it to his chest. A message is tied to its leg, which Dejunga unties. He then kisses the bird, throws it into the air, and watches it fly off toward the Sawnay Village. He unrolls the message: *The Boy with the Scar and other Yankees stayed in our village last night. They will travel north to the Black Swamp today.*

Dejunga and his braves will capture the boy and return to their village and give the boy to One Who Sees All. And for this, the Wendo will be rewarded with their return to Mother Earth, where they will wipe the Yankees from their ancestral land as he wiped the blood from the rock. That is, after they kill all the Sawnay men and enslave their lifegivers.

Dejunga grins, and among the Wendo, Dejunga is not known as a man who grins.

21

Back at the village, Sawnay were moving around as if they were doing their regular morning routines. People carried armfuls of firewood, others woven bark baskets laden with food. Everyone smiled warmly as I passed by, the stranger from another world, the world they'd left behind to avoid a shift that would've seen the end to their traditional way of life.

Children frolicked about, calling out in Sawnay. Dogs scampered and sniffed. At the entrances of dew-glistening tepees, women shook out heavy furs, reminding me of my mother shaking out damp linen on warm spring and summer days before she hung it on the line.

Still groggy, like they'd just woken up, Conroy and the others were sitting on a log bench outside the longhouse near a small fire that hadn't been burning when I left. The sun hadn't fully risen above the treetops surrounding the shaded village. It was noticeably cooler than it had been at the riverbank.

"Thought maybe you got yourself lost," said Colby, who was bent over wiping his Nikes clean again, only this time with a piece of hide.

I sat down next to Conroy, who had a fur draped over his shoulders like a cape. "Tabby told me what happened on the bluff," he said.

So much had happened that it took a moment for me to grasp what he was referring to. "Yeah, pretty crazy," I said.

"*Pretty crazy*, man, that was crazy times a hundred. No, no, no, make it a thousand," said Colby. "Crazy times a thousand—you flew like Superman."

"No, that was definitely more like Rambo," said Tabby. "*Rambo: First Blood.*"

"*Rambo: First Blood?*" said Conroy. "That movie's older than you."

Tabby shrugged and said, "I had to find out what the word Rambo meant . . . besides, it's a cult classic."

"You right, tomboy," said Colby, shaking his head in disbelief. "What girl watches Rambo?"

"Glooscap came right to our location," said Conroy. "Didn't seem surprised at all, as if he already knew we were there."

Simon handed me a bloated skin, and said, "Water."

I took a deep drink from the nipple.

"Where were you?" said Simon.

"The river," I said, passing the skin back.

"The river we crossed to get here?"

"It's full of dead fish," I said.

"You mean momma's milk?" said Colby. "We drank from it last night—tasted fine to me."

"I saw the unicorn colt too. Dead and floating downriver like the fish," I said. "Something's polluting it. Everyone who's traveled north to find the source hasn't returned."

"Are you serious?" said Tabby. "The *unicorn.*"

"That's some badass juju," said Colby. "*Lord of the Rings* shit right there."

"The Sawnay have a friend who lives two days north from here. His name's Ambrose," I said.

"Ambrose? That's an archaic name," said Anna.

"They say he's from Earth," I continued. "He taught the Sawnay English and maps and other stuff. They even know about North American borders. They said he can help us find a way home."

Colby leapt up, tossing the scrap of hide he'd been using to clean his shoes into the fire. "What are we waiting for then? Let's get this show on the road."

"How far is it?" said Simon calmly, like he was trying to offset Colby's excitement.

"Did he say it's for sure?" said Tabby.

"I don't know," I said, feeling foolish for not asking more questions.

Poowasan emerged from around a tepee along with Glixtan and Glooscap. They sat down across from Conroy.

"How would Tanner travel north with Glooscap?" said Conroy.

"Thunder horses," said Poowasan.

Hearing the word "horses" caused everyone to perk up. At that point, I'd yet to see any sign of horse whatsoever. There'd been nothing on the trail. Nothing in the village, none of the things you see or hear—or smell for that matter—no saddles, no tack, no harnesses, no corrals, no hoof tracks, no dung. There'd been no hooves pounding the earth, no neighs or bays or whinnies. Absolutely no sign at all. If the Sawnay owned horses, they didn't keep them in the village.

"What about the others?" said Conroy, his voice taking on that serious tone. "Can they go too?"

"The young men?" said Poowasan, looking at Simon and Colby.

"And my nieces," said Conroy.

Poowasan's brow furrowed and he gazed into the fire as if he was searching the flames for an answer, then he turned to the girls. "Two days' rough journey," he said. "One day through the forest on foot to reach the thunder horses, another day on horses to reach the heart of Black Swamp. North of there is where the Sawnay don't travel."

"Swamp, what kinda joker lives in a swamp?" said Colby. "And this guy's supposed to tell us how we get home. Man, it sounds hokier and hokier by the minute."

"They can all ride, taught them myself except for Tanner," said Conroy.

"Are there saddles?" said Tabby.

"No saddles—we ride bareback," said Glooscap.

"I've never ridden bareback before," said Anna.

"Me neither," said Simon.

"Ditto," said Tabby.

Colby gave his head a shake and turned to me. "You be the only one, cowboy."

I had, in fact, dozens of times at Whispering Cedars, and also a few times at Halton House. I could manage fine. The others, however, I wasn't so sure about.

"I'm not nearly ready to travel," said Conroy, raising his splinted leg a few inches off the ground. "Even with Glixtan's treatment."

"We can jerry-rig some type of stirrups," I said. "Or maybe a saddle of some type."

"Yeah, Mr. C.," said Colby. "No way we leaving you behind."

"I'll only slow you down," said Conroy.

"There's no way we're going unless you're going," said Tabby firmly.

"Uh-uh, we're not leaving without you," added Anna. "Me and Tabby will stay with you and wait for them to come back." She said it with a resoluteness that I'd never heard from her before. Then she and Tabby simultaneously sidled up on either side of Conroy, like what he proposed was opening a rift between them and the only way to stop it from widening farther was for each of them to hold on to one of his arms.

Simon looked at me. Together we looked at Colby. No one spoke. We didn't need to. We were all thinking exactly the same thing: Conroy was our leader, our father figure. He always made the right choices, always gave the best advice, and he'd been there for all of us whenever one of us needed someone to talk to, or someone to just listen to our teen-angst woes. Things like how we missed our family and friends, or how the world seemed to have been unfair toward us. Without him, traveling anywhere would be tough and downright frightening, especially in a world none of us knew anything about, a world in which danger was sure to confront us.

Sure, there'd been a few times that I'd grumbled and complained about my stay at Halton House, but that never lasted very long. My frustration subsided with the understanding that I'd made poor choices, put myself in bad situations. As a consequence, I'd hurt people, including myself. Conroy had helped me understand all of this, helping me gain more insight into how those traumatic events in my life—my father leaving, my mom and I moving around all the time, then her death—had impacted me and influenced my thoughts and feelings, my beliefs. Now, there he was, telling us that he wouldn't travel north with us to speak to this Ambrose—the only person it seemed—who knew the way home, the way home to Earth. I suddenly realized that I'd zoned out for a minute and hadn't been listening to the conversation going on around me.

"What if they don't come back?" said Anna. "I mean, they might not be able to, right? They might have to go on without us."

"No, they won't be going anywhere without you—you're going with them," said Conroy. "Both you and Tabitha."

Anna cast off her uncle's arm impulsively as though it had just zapped her. She leaned back. She stared at him with a mixture of anger, confusion, and fear, like he'd betrayed her but she wasn't quite sure how, like she could make him change his mind if she burned that look into him for long enough. I knew she wouldn't. She, like the others, must've known it as well.

"Will we be able to return for him?" said Simon. "I mean, after we talk to Ambrose."

Poowasan was silent for a moment too long before he said, "I am unsure."

"If something, if anything happens," said Conroy slowly. "If you need to hide, if you need to climb, if you need to move quickly—anything—I won't be able to keep up. I could jeopardize everyone. I can't afford that and neither can you."

"Can't afford that?" said Anna. She scoffed, stood up, and beelined into the heart of the village, tailed by one of the dogs. Everyone was silent as we watched her leaving.

Conroy picked up his crutches and went to go after her.

Tabby stood up and put a hand on his shoulder. "I'll go," she said. She trotted after her sister.

I thought I heard Conroy sigh, and that was the first time I could ever recall hearing him sigh. But then I'd experienced a lot of firsts over the last twenty-four hours. I got the feeling there were sure to be many more on that strange world none of us expected to be on yesterday—let alone knew existed—as we prepared for our basketball game against St. Michael's. A twenty-four hours which seemed so distant that it might as well have been a year ago. Who could've known? Who could've had an inkling that we'd be anywhere but Halton House where last night we would've helped Barley Charlie birth Hena's colt? Where, at that moment, we would've all been doing chores around the farm.

I gazed at the blue sky panning from side to side, wondering where Earth was up there, if it was up there anywhere. Those three planets had dimmed slightly. A few stubborn stars still clung on, flickering like sparks, the way they do right before they blink out. I admired those ones, always had because they were tenacious, didn't go easily. I wondered if any were our sun.

"Is the route dangerous?" said Conroy.

Poowasan's head swayed back and forth a few times, as if he was giving serious thought to the question, and then he said, "The Sawnay have traveled this way for generations. We know the land and the creatures who call it home. But this world suffers these days, and there are unknowns."

"Ambrose's home is safe," said Glooscap, who'd been silent up until that point.

"How's a swamp safe? Never heard that before," said Colby. "You got alligators, snakes, sinkholes, all sorts of crazy-ass bugs." He counted them off on his fingers.

"Boys, watch over Anna and Tabby. They're all right on horses, but they've spent most of their lives in the city. They aren't wise to the bush."

"We don't know anything about this world," said Simon. "Nothing about the animals. Don't know what's poisonous, what isn't. We almost ended up as bird food yesterday."

"Got to be crazy-ass jumbo rats, too, gnaw your eyes right out of your head," said Colby, still going off.

"That may be, but the Sawnay know it and you three are bright and world-smart," said Conroy. "Follow their lead. Keep your eyes open, trust your gut. Find us a way home."

"They leave before the day is fully born," said Poowasan with that same finality from the river. He said a few rapid words in Sawnay to Glooscap, who got to his feet and headed into the heart of the village in the direction the girls had gone. That was it. What minutes ago had seemed like a trip still days away, had materialized—almost too quickly.

Glooscap moved with purpose, his head high and shoulders back. There was a driving force in him that wanted all this to happen, like the cowboys or bull-riders I'd known: determined, focused, a belief in their ability, almost like they'd already accomplished what it was they were setting out to do. I admired that. And I gained a newfound respect for Glooscap right then and there.

"What if Ambrose can't help?" I said.

"I have asked Ambrose to help," said Poowasan. "He is a good friend of the Sawnay."

"What if we can't return? I mean . . . what if we have to make a choice?" I said, regretting it even before the words spilled from my mouth.

"Hang on, hang on," said Colby, crossing his arms over his chest. "Ain't any phones around here, man. How you go and tell this Ambrose to help us return?"

Poowasan smiled kindly as a parent would to a naive child, then he overlapped his wrists and fluttered his hands into the sky, and said, "A messenger."

Conroy leaned in closely to me. "You don't hesitate a second. The first chance you get to go home, you take it. I'll follow as soon as I can."

"We're not going without you," I said.

"Listen to me, Tanner," he said. "I'm responsible for all of you. You go the *first* chance you get. You boys and Anna and Tabby."

I didn't like the thought of being the one responsible for that decision. But what could I say that would change Conroy's mind, something that might persuade him that he was wrong this time, that we should all stick together, leave together? Nothing came to me, which left me wondering if it was because I just couldn't think of anything or if deep down I knew Conroy was right. We *should* go back the first chance we get. We *should* leave him behind because we might not get another chance. So I nodded, and he nodded in return.

22

As Poowasan spoke to Glixtan, we sat silently and watched the sun continue to rise above the treetops, the shade receding from the village by the second. Three small children kept peering curiously out from around a tepee. A woman appeared and uttered some words in Sawnay. She chased them off with a tree bough into the maze of tepees where they disappeared, only to reappear a few moments later from around another one. Their inquisitive eyes took us in, more determined than before, it seemed, to learn what was afoot in their village with the strange travelers in strange clothes who'd shown up the night before, the ones from Mother Earth.

"Why don't you move, just move to new land?" said Simon, tossing his head in a random direction. "Just leave and start over somewhere else?"

"Aren't there other places the Sawnay can settle?" I added.

Poowasan looked at me and I felt tiny again, like the night before when I was first brought into his presence. "I promised our people we would never leave. We have called this land home for eight generations since we left Mother Earth. This land we now sit on was picked by the elders of our village. This land has given the Sawnay all they need to grow. We have respected it like our own. Those Sawnay who have traveled on to the Spirit World are part of this land. We lose all of this if we leave."

I took in the awakening village, the cheerful voices and laughter. Somewhere, a baby cried, looking to be fed. The young, the old, and the in-between carried on with their daily routines. It was a living, breathing community. It was a place where people were born, where they grew up, where they fell in love, where they raised children and shared time with family and friends. And it was where they celebrated life, and where they mourned death.

All of it would be destroyed if a cure for Cootamain wasn't found. I could remember watching the stories of oil companies that owned and operated oil rigs in third-world countries in Africa and South America. Pipelines would often rupture and bleed their oil into pristine rainforest rivers near villages that'd been there for hundreds of years. The villagers would continue to fish, drink, and wash from the toxin-filled water out of necessity. What about Alberta, Canada, to the north? I remembered the story I'd watched about toxins from tailings ponds leaching into the Athabasca River. A river that First Nations communities relied on for sustenance, and I remembered fish with filmy eyes, people getting sick. The poison in Cootamain, like a metastasizing cancer, would slowly kill it, like the lung cancer that ate my grandfather away to nothing, before taking his life. Unless Glooscap and the others discovered what was causing the poison and found a way to stop it, the Sawnays' way of life would end. It was just a matter of time.

I tried to think what it would be like if I had to leave a place that I lived my entire life, a place my family had been for eight generations. But then I'd never known life at one spot. I'd never been able to plant myself in one location and root some roots. For the majority of my life, I bounced from one place to the next. The longest my mother and I stayed anywhere was at Vince's ranch, and that was only two years. After my father left, we lived in low-rental apartments or highway motels on the outskirts of small towns I could no longer remember the names of, towns that blurred together like the miles of dusty, tumbleweed-strewn highway my mother and I had driven along. Towns where I attended school for a few months, always trying to fit in as the new guy, while my mother worked some dead-end job as a waitress at a café or a cashier at a drugstore. Then when a tornado swept across some place like Texas or Oklahoma or a hurricane hit Florida or Louisiana, my mother's phone rang, and she always, always answered and made plans with whoever it was on the other end of the line. I tried to recall what I'd seen more of vanish on the horizon—the rear end of my mother's Ford Mustang as she drove away on one of her storm chases, or those indistinguishable towns as we hit the road again, striking out for a new destination, uncertain of our future, poignantly aware of our past.

I always thought that I ought to be sad as we were leaving, but I never was. I guess we did so much of it that I got used to it. Standing there, I understood why the Sawnay couldn't simply uproot and move somewhere else, but I couldn't feel why.

Glooscap appeared, walking with the older, round-faced woman from the previous night who'd handed us the berries and juice-skin in the longhouse. And like the previous night, she smiled warmly as she approached us, friendly and inviting; I could even say motherly.

"Weesan will help you prepare for the journey," said Glooscap.

Out of the corner of my eye, I saw Anna and Tabby coming toward us. Anna no longer looked upset. I wondered what Tabby had said to soothe her: Don't worry we'll come back for him? If we can't, he'll follow as soon as he can travel? These were the types of things that I'd probably say. Weesan approached the girls and began gesturing for them to follow her. When she noticed us boys weren't coming, she stopped and said, "You come with."

We got up and went to follow.

"Tanner, stay back a minute," said Conroy, gesturing his head to the seat beside him.

The others didn't seem to hear. They kept walking without glancing back. I sat down. As the others rounded a tepee, Anna turned back to give us a wave before disappearing.

We sat quietly for a minute as the noise of the village steadily increased, like an awakening heartbeat, voices and barks echoing off the hides. Then Conroy locked his gray eyes on me, that serious look he gave when he passed on advice. "I want you to know that I trust your judgment fully, completely. You're going to need to rely on it now more than ever before, Tanner."

"We can bring you with us. We'll just ride slower," I said, not liking where this was going. That rift I imagined opening up between him and the girls earlier started to open between us.

"Tanner," he said sighing, shaking his head. "If something happened and you needed to hustle . . ."

Hearing him so openly admit his weakness was upsetting. To see him physically broken was hard. At the same time, it gave me an even deeper respect for a man who I knew was capable of pretty much anything. A lump started to build at the back of my throat.

"Watch over them like your brothers and sisters," said Conroy. "You're all in this together. You'll need each other. They'll listen to you."

"They're not going to listen to me. What I say doesn't matter."

"Give them friendship, something they've been missing most of their lives—even my nieces. They'll listen then. Being a leader isn't commanding—"

"It's inspiring," I said, finishing a quote that I'd learned from him. "But we have so many differences."

"That's a strength. Those differences are a strength. See the possibilities, not the limitations. If the opportunity to go home arises, make *sure* you take it."

"We're not leaving without—"

"*Tanner*, you go if you get the chance. Don't let Anna or Tabby talk you out of it—you all go, you hear me?"

With those last words, I felt like the tie holding us together had been severed. What was ahead for us? At that point, I had no idea. I couldn't begin to imagine, with everything that had already happened. Who could? I knew what was in the past. I spent my entire life thinking about it, wishing I could somehow turn around and change those things that seemed to define me, make different choices with those ones that I knew had been wrong, and try to get my parents to make different choices, too.

I looked at Conroy, and knew an oath, a vow, a commitment had been made between us.

I spotted the others coming back. They had changed into deer hide clothing, which took away their modern American look. If I saw them at a distance, I would've thought they were Sawnay, except maybe for Colby, as dark as he was. He and Tabby had hide bundles slung over their shoulders. Anna had her Gucci purse instead, Simon his gym bag.

"What do you think?" said Anna, turning sideways to strike a pose.

"I think you're having way too much fun," said Tabby. She stuck her finger in her throat. Anna backhanded her shoulder.

"What?" said Tabby. "You tried on like ten pairs. Then you tried to change *again* before we left. Then you wanted my shirt—that's why I don't shop with you or Mom. That's why I get up an hour before you to use the bathroom. You're a prima donna of the highest order."

Anna ignored her sister and sat down in between Conroy and me to put her hair in a ponytail. I pictured Anna in the bathroom for hours, door locked, applying make-up, and straightening her long shiny brown hair with the straightener that she always packed around everywhere in her purse with all the other girly stuff.

Over one of Glooscap's shoulders was a bundle. On the other, he carried a sheath full of red-fletched arrows and an unstrung bow made of a rust-colored wood. Following him were Cawop and Broden, both carrying their own bundles, bows and arrows. Glooscap's fierce eyes had returned as if he was again possessed, like he eagerly awaited what lay ahead, whatever it may be.

Those three mischievous children reappeared around a tepee. They watched me a moment, then they smiled and waved. Smiling, I waved back and they darted into the maze of tepees, shouting something out in Sawnay as they left. All of this would be gone— long gone—if Glooscap and the others weren't successful. Right then, a part of me wished I could join them, help them in some way. But what more could I offer? I was just a kid from another world, without any idea of how this new world worked. Heck, I barely knew how my own world worked. I'd be more of a hindrance than a help.

We were all sitting on the benches around the fire, outside of the longhouse. Poowasan and the other Sawnay were in a heated discussion, gesturing with their hands, as if they were going over plans of great importance.

"Girls, this is for the best," said Conroy softly.

"We're not going home without you," said Anna.

"Now listen, I want all of you guys to stick together," said Conroy.

"No way, we ain't leaving you, Mr. C.," said Colby.

As Conroy nodded his head, his mouth stretched thin and he shut his eyes like he did when he heard something he didn't agree with, but knew it wasn't the time or place to argue.

"You just did that thing you do when you don't agree," said Tabby, pointing a finger at him.

"He did too," said Anna.

Conroy reached out a hand to Anna, but she leaned away and she looked at me accusingly. "You two already talked about this when we were gone," she said. "Didn't you?"

My face flushed. She huffed like she was disgusted.

"If we do find a way home, he can follow us later," said Simon, trying to help out.

Anna whirled at him, and yelled, "How do you know?"

He didn't respond.

"Exactly, you don't know. You don't know anything, Simon—so don't even butt in into this."

"Like I said before, I'll only be a burden," said Conroy.

"He's right," I said quietly. I didn't like it, but it was the truth. "If the Sawnay hadn't found you guys on the slope yesterday, you'd all be dead."

"But his leg feels better," said Tabby, looking at her uncle. "You said so yourself last night." Her voice was pleading.

"Not better enough," he said.

Tabby stood up and looked to Poowasan for support. "Tell them it's safe. You said it's safe, the trip to see your friend. It's past the swamp that's not safe, right?"

"Tabby, please listen to me," soothed Conroy, reaching for her hand. She backed away out of range.

"The journey is safer the faster one travels," said Poowasan. "Your uncle will be a guest of the Sawnay until he returns to Mother Earth."

"What if he never returns?" said Anna. "What then?"

No one spoke.

Sniffling, Tabby wiped a hand across her eyes. That was the second time I'd seen her cry since we arrived. Carol's death, now this. In fact, I never thought she would. She seemed so much different than Anna, who I'd stumbled upon crying twice before. Both times while she'd been talking with someone on her iPhone, once in the hay barn—and I mean bawling—and another time when we were all shopping at Walmart. I'd went back out to the van to grab the coupons Carol had forgotten and found Anna inside, wiping tears from her eyes with a Kleenex, her phone pressed to her ear. I thought it was boyfriend trouble with some guy from San Francisco, the one she always gabbed about, and who Tabby always poked fun at, saying he had short-man syndrome. It all made sense now, with those text messages that I read on the bluff. I couldn't help but glance at her stomach, but just like last time, I couldn't find any sign of her unborn baby.

"What if he can't follow us? What if he never returns? What then?" said Tabby, repeating her sister's questions.

This statement caused Anna to wrap her arms around her uncle, bury her head into his shoulder, and begin to cry.

"What if all this just a bunch of mumbo-jumbo?" said Colby.

I figured every one of us was aware that it was a real possibility we might never return to Earth, never see Halton House again, never see Hena's colt, never watch movies, never eat pizza or enjoy ice cream. We might never hear our favorite bands—no iPhones, no

Facebook, no YouTube, no Levis, no cars, no trucks, and definitely no bookstores or libraries. And what about our family? Nothing at all. Without it, what would life be like? Like the Stone Age, that was what it would be like. Simple or difficult? Who knew for certain? The farthest I'd been away from civilization was those two years I spent at Whispering Cedars. But during that time, there'd been trips to town for shopping, school during the weekdays. There'd been the amenities of modern society, playing Xbox with the ranch hands, watching movies on weekends, listening to classic rock on my iPod or blaring from the Kenwood house speakers in the big shop. There'd been all of that, and then some.

Tabby dropped her bundle and rushed forward into her uncle's arms. He wrapped both his nieces tightly in an embrace. It dawned on me that this could very well be the last time Conroy, Anna, and Tabby would ever hold one another, could be the last time they would ever see one another.

Poowasan started chanting softly, and the other Sawnay joined in, as if it was a song they all knew well. It was simple, and soon Simon also joined in and then I did too, and finally even Colby. We all chanted along. It felt like a song that I'd known my entire life. I tried to place it but couldn't quite put my finger on it.

Being there with everyone and chanting like that, it was beautiful. I'd never done anything like it before, except maybe Christmas caroling once or twice. But this was different. How? I don't know exactly. It brought us together there, and it was soothing. After a few moments, neither I nor the others had any difficulty keeping rhythm. And when it did start to fade, everyone seemed to be calmer, as if they all begrudgingly accepted the decision to leave Conroy behind while we journeyed north to see Ambrose. The girls released their uncle, both gazing up at him as if he was at the top of some great height.

Could there've been more to our final hour before embarking on that journey? Maybe, people waving to us as we left the village, more round faces like Weesan's, more kind words, words of encouragement in English or Sawnay or both. Maybe like the romantic images that I'd seen of young men as they prepared to head off to fight in WWI or II, or like the townsfolk wishing good luck to hired guns who were riding out to hunt down a gang of outlaws in those Western novels that I'd been reading since I was a boy. For us, there was none of that. There was no pomp, no extravagance, no type of going-away ceremony.

Colby handed me a bundle and a set of deer hides. I went into the longhouse to change, a place that still felt safe and welcoming. A part of me wanted to curl back up under the fur to sleep the morning away, forget everything for just a while longer, perhaps wake up from this dream, if it was a dream.

I changed into the hides, leaving my torn, mud-stained clothes near the cushion I'd sat on. They weren't a bad fit. A little heavy and constricting, not what you'd want to play basketball in, but they were somewhat comfortable, in a frontiersman-like way.

Outside, Poowasan spoke with Glooscap. The others were in a half circle around Conroy. I walked over and slung the bundle Colby had given me onto my shoulder, like it was the gym bag that I'd been carrying to all those basketball games against St. Michael's, only this wasn't a game. There were no referees, no penalties, no buzzers, no scoreboards, no Mr. Wilkes standing on the sidelines, and no fans cheering or booing for that matter. This was as real as it could get. More real than I wanted it to be.

"Not a bad fit," said Simon, nodding.

Cawop pointed at Colby's Nikes, which clashed against his hide pants, and said, "Those moccasins—powerful medicine." And with those words, I noticed for the first time how guttural his voice was, as if his voice box was more animal than human. The skin on my neck pricked. "You want to trade?" said Cawop. He put his foot forward and lifted his pant leg to reveal a tan moccasin that looked about a thousand miles overdue for a change.

"Man, these are the finest shoes I ever owned," said Colby. "Only way someone getting them is by taking them off my dead body."

A solemnness swept through the group. Then Anna's chin started quivering, on the verge of another crying bout. The girls had never known the deep hurt from profound loss to the degree that we boys had, the degree that burns your nerve endings dead, makes it so you doubt the world around you and don't expect a whole lot of good to come your way ever again. Like when my father left, leaving me with all those unanswered questions. Some of which my mother knew the answers for but would never get a chance to reveal, because she took them with her to Oklahoma, where that F5 tornado took her away forever.

Then it hit me. My father had been gone for ten years, almost to the day. What were the chances both of us vanishing from our lives around the same day? There'd been so many changes after he left, with all of the confusion, uncertainty, grief, chaos, and turbulence in my and my mother's life—all that and more. She and I had driven down lonely, dusty highways, searching hotels, motels, and honky-tonks, both waiting—and praying to a god who never seemed to listen—for her cellphone to ring, for that spark of hope that never came, a spark we so desperately needed for our lives to be complete again, for that void to be filled or at least the hope of it to be. A spark that would've stopped her tears from soaking her pillow every night. Because we were incomplete after he left. Although I was only seven at the time, I knew a vital piece had been torn from our lives, and that made it impossible for us to be complete. And my mother, well, my mother started spending more and more time away from home, more time away from me. Different men came and went. Or maybe we came and went, would be more accurate. It was like she was as restless as the storms she spent her life chasing. Just when I found myself getting comfortable with one of her new boyfriends, she packed us up and we moved again. The fighter pilot, Chip. Brad the ironworker who walked steel beams fifty stories in heavy winds above cities like New York and Dubai. Will the park ranger who watched over Colorado National Park, saving animals, arresting poachers. Even after my mother met Vince and we moved to Whispering Cedars, her cellphone would ring and she'd take off to storm-chase in some other state. I'd arrive home from school to find Vince preparing dinner by himself, usually medium-rare steak, baked potatoes, and Greek salad, his favorite meal which had become my favorite. Vince would pat me on the back, ask how my day went, then say something like, "Sorry, bud, she couldn't wait until you got home. She'll be back in a few days though. Maybe sooner." But he and I both knew it never ended up being just a few days, more often like a week, sometimes two. It happened so many times over the years that I got used to it, as an aging athlete got used to defeat. Then, that previous March, she never returned home.

As I came out of my thoughts, Conroy kissed Anna and Tabby's foreheads and whispered to them. Glooscap and the other Sawnay stood by the fire, gazing at the brilliant alien sun in the north, as if they were eager to leave.

"We'll find a way home," said Simon. "I know we will."

"I bet my bottom dollar on it," said Conroy.

I thought maybe Anna or Tabby might start pleading with their uncle again, but they didn't. Conroy let go of the girls and shook Colby's hand, then Simon's. When it came to my turn, his jaw muscle knotted and then he took my hand with the firmest handshake I'd ever felt. We didn't speak. There was no need. We'd discussed all there was to discuss. He nodded and let my hand go.

Glooscap and his men were patiently standing in a circle, speaking in hushed Sawnay to one another like they were worried the sound of their voices might interrupt our farewell. That was it. We were leaving. What did I feel? At the time, a tempest of things, I guess— fear, excitement, hope, boldness, and adventurous and of course trepidation. All of that and more, I was sure. Something that seemed so distant a few hours ago, and something that would've been totally unbelievable a few days ago, was happening right then and there.

We were about to embark on a journey that was like a quest in a novel or movie. Sure, I'd been along for an imaginary ride on more times than I could count, but then that had been fiction, with no real chance of injury or death. Wondering what the others were thinking, I took a moment and studied the party. We were all from different walks of life. Three boys who'd had a fling with the law, two rich girls, and three real-deal Sawnay right out of the sixteenth century— what a motley group we were.

"This is for you," said Glixtan. He'd come right up beside me without a sound. He reached out his hand. When I put my hand out, he ceremoniously placed a tiny black stone in my palm. I was hit by déjà vu. Touching my chest, I felt the medicine pouch that the old Indian had given me the night before at the Shell. It held the stone that heated up yesterday and last night, warning me of danger.

I clutched the leather thong and removed the pouch from under my hide shirt. I loosened the drawstring and dumped the stone into my hand. They were identical beside each other. Glixtan nodded, giving me a mischievous smile, his eyes twinkling.

"Wait, where . . . how do you have the same stone?" I said mystified, shaking my head, trying to make sense of it all.

"Life is full of unknowns, of mystery," he whispered. He touched his temple with a finger, then his heart, then his temple again. "Believe in yourself on the longest journey." And like the stone, the gesture was also the same from the night before. Perplexed, I waited for him to say more, but he turned and hobbled over to Poowasan. I took a final look at the stones, then rolled them into the pouch, and dropped it back down my shirt.

"Hang on a sec," I said to Glixtan. I rushed over to Simon and went into his gym bag while he was talking to Conroy. *All the Pretty Horses* was still inside. I picked it up and headed back over to Glixtan, handed it to him, feeling a trade was due, like two nights before at the Shell, the Root Beer for the medicine pouch.

He examined the book cover. "*All the Pretty Horses*," he said slowly. "Thank you, Tanner."

"Are you ready?" said Glooscap to all of us.

Conroy gave us the thumbs-up. When his nieces stood from the bench to pick up their bundles, he dug inside his pocket. "Here, Tanner, might come in handy." He removed his Swiss Army knife.

I went to take it but he held on for a second. "This was my father's," he said. "I'd like it back. Tanner, remember—what anger wants, it buys at the price of soul." Then he let the knife go, and I slipped it into the kangaroo pouch on the front of my shirt.

"Man, you gonna lose that knife just like her phone," said Colby.

"Well, we better get a move on," I said, changing the subject.

"Where's these thunder horses at?" said Colby. "Better be some fine animals, no broken-down old mules or ponies."

"The way you ride, it won't matter," said Simon jokingly.

Glooscap pointed toward the sun, which had risen fully above the treetops, bathing the village in light. "We need to go to them. We will arrive before night falls."

Everyone was silent. I guess there was nothing more left to say. And so that was how we started off on our journey, walking in a single file through the village like we had the night before, only this time we weren't prisoners. This time, we were equals.

23

Without caution, we entered the forest on the same trail Glooscap and I had taken earlier that morning, the fog having dissipated. I reflexively glanced at my heels, thinking that mangy, one-eyed dog might be lopping behind me. But it wasn't there.

I didn't look back for a final view of the village. I'd had a hard time looking back in the rear view ever since my Uncle Hanker and I had left Whispering Cedars on that long, gravel driveway leading to Highway 101. The tires of his Lincoln kicked up a dust plume that billowed and stretched for miles, twisting and swirling out over the fields. I'd wondered then if that was what my mother had seen in those final moments in Oklahoma, right before that F5 tornado engulfed her friend's truck, right before she saw nothing at all. Leaving Whispering Cedars that day, tears streaked down my cheeks—the last time I cried—down into the corners of my mouth, tears I hid from my uncle by looking back at a place that had started to feel like home. That day, an emptiness had opened up inside of me and converged with that other emptiness, from losing my mother and father. It was like the world I thought I knew was simply a naive illusion, like the world I'd believed in for my entire life had been a lie. Like it was a deception I myself had unwittingly helped to create and foster with all of my hope and belief in those people that I thought I could trust, those promises that had been made and broken over and over and over.

The village's lively sounds began to fade as we headed north on a trail to a destination none of us knew existed yesterday. Once in a while, Glooscap sped up seemingly unconsciously, as if he was itching to move faster. But then he caught himself, paused to look back, and waited for the others.

Eventually, we crossed Cootamain on a log bridge that could've been the one from the night before, if we'd been traveling south instead of north. We hiked up a winding forest trail that ran alongside another river, narrow and swiftly moving, which Glooscap told us fed into Cootamain.

A few hours or so after the bridge, I heard labored breaths beside me. "We used to hike in Northern California every spring break with our parents," said Anna. "This kinda reminds me of it."

"Never been," I said "But I've seen pictures of the redwoods."

"That was before Dad took a new job at the bank," said Tabby, who'd joined us. "Before he started traveling all the time for work."

"That's why we're staying with our uncle—Mom and Dad had to fly over to Greece for the bank Dad works for," said Anna. "He's way up there on the totem pole."

"Oh, come on," said Tabby, sighing. "Mom didn't have to go. She doesn't like leaving San Francisco. She doesn't like leaving us. It's because she thinks Dad's humping that bimbo, Francine. That's why she wouldn't let him go by himself."

"So not true," said Anna testily. "Mom's just tired of hearing Dad complain about how lonely he is when he travels."

"He says he's lonely so she won't think he's having an affair," said Tabby.

"You guys see that?" said Simon. He pointed off to our left where the forest was thicker. All I could see were tree trunks and other flora.

"What are you talking about?" said Colby.

Everyone stopped dead on the trail.

"Animals," said Simon. "Coming this way."

A trickle of animals emerged from the forest, a few deer, a black bear and her cubs, followed by six or seven wolves. All seemingly oblivious of one another, oblivious of us. Then the entire forest erupted in a maelstrom. Snapping branches, crashes in the undergrowth, thudding sounds, and then a menagerie of animals burst from the trees. They stampeded toward us as if they were being chased by something, something menacing, something ferocious and deadly that terrified them to the core. Two large, tanned cats that resembled cougars shot past the other animals, past us, chased by a herd of deer, then raccoons and porcupines and possums, and other small animals I'd never seen before. And even birds. Hundreds of birds blasted from the canopy. Enough animals to fill Noah's Ark, it seemed. Only as far as I could tell, it wasn't a flood they were fleeing.

24

We were all stunned, unsure of what to do next. Then Glooscap yelled out in Sawnay, snapping us out of our frozen states just as a black mass of insects—beetles the size of small dogs—surged from the undergrowth. Dozens, hundreds, then thousands. Heading straight toward us, they overran the slower moving animals.

"To the rocks," screamed Glooscap, pointing at a formation of high rocks on the other side of the river. Everyone bolted toward the riverbank, splashed into the water crazily, and started thrashing across. It was waist deep. The icy cold caused me to gasp, robbing my breath momentarily and shriveling my gonads to the size of raisins. My feet slipped on the smooth river rocks, almost sending me splashing into the current. I used my arms like paddles to pull my body forward.

The stampede of animals headed down the trail in the direction from which we came. The beetles continued to surge toward us, on both sides of the river, like an indomitable force of nature. Their carapaces were oily purple. Their pinchers snapped the air greedily, as the incessant ticking sound they made grew louder and louder with every passing second. I suddenly dropped to chest depth. Colby went down next, bobbed back up, and struggled to regain his footing before he righted himself to carry on. Everyone else made it across without incident. At least that was what I thought.

When I reached the opposite bank, a loud splash sounded behind me. Anna was the only one who wasn't with us. I turned back to see her spinning and trashing in the current, being carried quickly downriver, her Gucci purse bobbing behind her, like a million-dollar buoy, about to become a million-dollar anchor.

Then I saw it. A plume of mist was rising up high above the river some ways down, a waterfall. My heart leapt, remembering the waterfall that cascaded into that vast canyon. I wondered how high this drop was. This edge was sixty, maybe seventy feet away. It had to be a good drop to create a mist like that.

The others hadn't noticed that Anna and I were no longer with them. They had climbed the bank. They were running toward the rocks, their sopping clothes draping like wet blankets.

The beetles' clicking noise drowned out the sounds of the river and Anna's garbled cries. The mass reached a bend, flowing over the banks to bob like giant corks before scuttling atop the surface heading directly toward me. Animal bones lay picked clean, from the ones that had been overrun, and then devoured.

What lay at the bottom of that waterfall—jagged rocks, rapids, a gnarly logjam? I had no idea. But I knew Anna would learn firsthand if I didn't do something, both her and her unborn baby.

I glanced at the others. They were climbing the rocks, still unaware we weren't with them. Then, I turned and dove into the river. I swam furiously after Anna. She floundered about, getting farther and farther away from me, closer and closer to the waterfall, nearer and nearer to death.

Swimming with the current helped me against the burden of my wet and cumbersome bundle and hide clothes. Then I was behind her, snatching at her in hopes to grab a hold. I missed twice before I grabbed her arm and slowed her down. Together, we fought toward the bank, which was a steep six feet high at that point. With my free hand, I scrabbled for a handhold, coming away with only dirt. Thorny brambles festooned down the bank into the river. I seized a handful, the thorns piercing my palm, sending a stinging pain shooting up through my arm. All the while, the current pulled mercilessly at our bodies, wet clothes, and Anna's monstrous purse.

"Let go of the purse," I yelled.

"What are we going to do?" she cried out.

Up river, hundreds of beetles blanketed the surface, getting closer by the second. Hundreds more poured over the bank. Even if we could climb up before they reached us, there was no way we could've reached the rocks. There wasn't enough time. They would've overrun us like they did to the animals, and left our bones picked clean, too.

"How long can you hold your breath?" I said.

Her eyes widened, and I started to count: "One, two," and on "three" we both took deep lungful of air and dunked under, just as the beetles arrived at our location.

I'd never actually timed how long I could hold my breath. But that day, I started to count in my mind. At the tenth count, I felt legs skittering over my head and shoulders. I opened my eyes to look at the surface. There was no light above us, only blackness, so I shut my eyes again. At thirty, I sensed the beetles above us still. At one hundred, my lungs started to burn and I had to use all my will to stay under, to hold out for as long as I could. I prayed Anna was managing to hold on. Beetles or not, we'd have to surface. So I wanted to stretch out as many of those precious seconds as possible. When my lungs began to convulse, I exploded from the water, gasping for air, prepared for beetles to swarm me, for their pinchers to tear the flesh from my face. But, except for a few stragglers, they were gone.

Voices hollered in the distance, but I couldn't make out what they were saying, nor could I see the others.

"We made it," said Anna, breathing heavily, her face red. "I can't believe we made it."

"*Up* the bank—*up, up, up,*" I pulled her in close to the bank. "Here, you go first. Careful, there's thorns."

She tried to take a hold of the brambles, but as soon as she touched them she snapped her hand back. "I can't. They're too big."

"Stand on my shoulders then," I said. "You should be able to reach the top."

Holding onto the thorny, biting brambles with one hand, Anna with the other, I knelt down into river until only my head was above the surface, water sloshing in my mouth and nose.

She slung her waterlogged purse around her back. She climbed onto my shoulders, and leaning up against the bank, she stood shakily to her feet. She grabbed a hold of the top, and then half-pulled, half-jumped, kicking me directly in the nose with her heel, as her sister had done in the van. Then she was up and over.

"Ouch," I yelled, my eyes watering.

She peeped over the edge, hand to her mouth. "Sorry. Here, let me help."

"No, just get back." Clutching the brambles, I pulled myself up the bank, the wet hides weighing me down like a ton of concrete. The beetles were gone from the high ground as well. No sign they'd been there except for the bone yard they left behind.

Atop the rock, the others were leaping up and down, waving and shouting triumphantly at us, as if their favorite team had just scored the winning goal.

"Anna, Tanner," yelled Tabby. "You scared the hell out of us."

"Thought you were din-din," yelled Colby. "Man, you like a cat with nine lives." He smiled his toothy smile.

"We thought you two went over the edge," said Simon.

"We held our breath," said Anna, shaking her arms to shed water.

Anna and I began to trudge toward them, our wet clothes leaving a snail trail. Glooscap was the first to meet us, and he clasped my forearm and shook it vigorously.

Anna and Tabby went into each other's arms to hug.

"How is it that Tabby's a competitive swimmer, and you can't swim?" said Colby.

"I can swim," said Anna, giving Colby fierce eyes that rivaled Glooscap's. "Just not as good as her." Her hands were on her hips.

"If you can swim, then I can fly," he scoffed.

"I've never seen dodas in a swarm," said Glooscap. "They travel alone and only at night."

"If an ecosystem's being damaged, its inhabitants might act strangely," said Simon.

"He's right," said Anna. "Maybe the poison in Cootamain."

"Upsetting the balance," I added.

Brodan nodded as though what we'd said made total sense.

Anna took my hand to examine where the thorns had pierced my palm. It bled freely. "Why didn't you say anything?" she said.

"Didn't think it was the right time or place," I said.

Glooscap slid his bundle around to his stomach and dug inside. He removed a small tan pouch, like the one Glixtan used the night before in the longhouse. He removed some thin strips of hide to use for bandages. "This will help to heal the wounds." He handed them to Anna.

"Tabby, help me," she said. She opened the pouch and dumped some of the contents into my palm, a fine white powder like chalk dust. Then she and Tabby wrapped the strips around my hand and tied them tightly.

"Tonight, we eat doda," said Cawop enthusiastically, approaching the group. He swung a doda at his side by the pinchers, like a rabbit by its feet. A red-fletched arrow stuck out of its carapace.

No one said anything: Everyone just gave him a dumbfounded look, like was he really serious? He wants us to eat a giant alien beetle for dinner? He stopped dead in his tracks, ten feet away from us. There followed a heavy silence over the next few seconds as he shifted from enthusiastic, to confused, to finally grasping that no one was craving doda.

"You know what, let's give it a taste," I said, feeling bad for him.

"No way I'm eating bugs," said Colby, vehemently shaking his head.

"They're a delicacy in some countries," said Anna.

"Not in San Fran," said Tabby.

Colby scoffed and said, "Yeah, not in Detroit either." He gave Tabby a fist bump. "What about you, Simon?"

"My people don't eat insects," said Simon too quick.

Disappointed, Cawop turned with his catch and headed over to the riverbank. He dropped the doda to the ground, stepped on it, tugged the arrow loose, and then tossed his idea of lunch fare into the water, where it landed with a splash. Everyone laughed. And with this laughter, the gravity of what had happened moments ago vanished along with the mass of flesh-eating beetles.

Over the next little while, we changed into the extra hide clothing that we'd brought with us. We wrung out our wet clothes and laid them out on the rocks to dry. Colby's Air Maxes hadn't looked so clean since the day he bought them. We relaxed in the shade, snacking on fruit and dried meat, as the forest returned to normal.

After the sun dried our clothes, we packed up our bundles and started off again. We followed the trail along the river a ways north for the better part of an hour, then crossed it using some boulders to follow the trail again single file.

25

The longer we were on that new world, and the more that I saw, the more I recognized elements from Earth, as if Earth had inherited certain qualities, as a child inherits eye color, shape of hand, traits, and mannerisms from his or her parents. But then that made sense, because the Sawnay had called the World of Dawn Earth's mother, and so maybe everything on Earth came from the planet we were now on. I remembered thinking to myself, what else did that world have in store for us? We'd only been there for a day—towering trees, enormous birds, unicorns, and a swarm of giant beetles. If someone from another world were to visit Earth for one day, they'd only see an iota of what lived on the planet, maybe only a small fraction of an iota. And so why would it be any different for us here?

Who knew? Who knew what lies ahead? If I were to jump ahead a week or a month to carry on with the story, nothing would make sense to anyone. And so I won't. You'll just have to listen patiently as it unfolds.

We resumed our steady pace, the line stretching out long, and at other times tightening. I had ample opportunity to ask myself many more questions, things like: Who else lived here? Were there more people from Earth? How big was the planet? Were there more villages, or towns, or cities? I stored them away hoping Glooscap or Ambrose would be able to answer them at some point.

Come late afternoon, we reached a wide, flat rock that ran into the river like a ramp. Glooscap said we would stop to rest awhile.

Scattered over the rock were shell fragments. Glooscap knelt down and cupped water to his mouth to drink.

I picked up a handful of shells. They were like acorn shells, only fragile from exposure. There were a few river-washed stones, which I picked up and dropped into my kangaroo pouch.

"Whatcha gonna do with those?" said Colby.

I removed one of the stones, then stood and rolled it in my hand until it felt right. I winged it at a tree. It thumped the trunk dead center.

"Let me guess, you learned it on the farm?" he said.

"Birds smash open the shells on this rock. They eat the meat inside, use the shells for nests. World of Dawn provides all for her children," said Glooscap.

I thought of blenders, microwaves, flat-screen TVs, cellphones and notepads, game systems, and all the other man-made devices that I'd been using most of my life, up until yesterday. The Sawnay didn't have any of it, but life carried on anyway. Kneeling down beside Glooscap, I removed the skin from my bundle to fill it from the creek. He looked back at the others. "We need to travel faster," he said uncharacteristically low, low enough that no one else heard.

"Not everyone can move like us," I said, noticing Brodan and Anna—she, breathing heavily and him, carrying her Gucci—walking beside each other. She was flushed, locks of hair hung across her face. Trying to decide what I thought about him carrying her purse, I took another drink from the creek. Why hadn't she asked me?

Simon snapped his head around to look north up the trail, as though he might've heard a sound but wasn't quite sure. "Did you hear that?"

"You have good ears," said Glooscap. "They sense our arrival."

Brodan spoke in Sawnay, nodding to Simon, and smiling for the first time since I'd met him. Glooscap and Cawop chuckled and said a few words to each other.

"What'd you say?" said Simon inquisitively, eyes wide, like he thought maybe he'd been the brunt of a joke.

"I said your Indian spirit is still strong," said Brodan. He patted Simon on the shoulder to assure him he meant no harm.

"He also said you remind him of his brother," said Glooscap.

"Man, you got elephant ears, Simon," said Colby. "You'd think all that music would beat up your eardrums, but no way. I bet you hear a mouse fart a mile away."

Tabby finished filling her waterskin. She was composed, as if she hadn't been hiking all morning. From what I'd seen, she seemed to be in her element, the outdoors. I'd never seen this side of her before, and I felt a newfound admiration toward her. Out of all the others, she looked to be the most unstrained, like she was taking it all in stride.

Even though we only met the Sawnay yesterday, and we were from different cultures—five hundred years apart—I could sense a camaraderie forming between our two parties. We were united, brought together by a mystery too complex to solve, a riddle too complicated to answer—us by a need to return home, and them driven by a need to save their home. The one common denominator: a need to survive. Earlier, Brodan and Cawop had started talking with the others in English, and I'd even heard a few laughs on the trail. Everyone was lowering those personal walls, no longer so suspicious of one another.

Not long after we set off again, we came to a steep part of the trail. Twisty roots as thick as a person's arm protruded from the hillside, running down the trail like arteries. We hiked slowly over the next half hour, navigating up through the tangled root system, all the while neighs and whinnies—unmistakable and so very comforting—grew increasingly distinct and louder. They were sounds that I heard in my daydreams, in my nightdreams, sounds that brought me comfort, wrapping me in an inviting blanket of memory. Those sounds were like a mellifluous song that I'd known my entire life, which only sounded better each time I heard it. I'd been around horses all my life, been around those sounds since even before I could remember. My father had made his living as a first-rate bronco buster, and my grandfather as a cowboy.

"They don't sound like broken-down mules or ponies," said Colby from behind me, relief in his voice.

"No broken-down mules or ponies—thunder horses," said Glooscap.

26

I crested the ridge right behind Glooscap to see a small glen with a dozen or so large painted horses, their musculature clearly visible. Some were prancing about, tossing their manes, swishing their tails, while others were drinking from a crystal-clear stream, that divided the glen, or grazing on bountiful patches of long grass. A few paused and turned to look curiously at Glooscap and me. The rest of the group hadn't yet arrived on the top of the ridge. Strangely, I felt like I'd been there before. Maybe I'd once seen a similar setting in a picture or on TV or in a movie.

A powerful stallion, all black save a few patches of white, lifted his head from the stream. He stared at us for a moment, water dripping from his muzzle. Waving his head back and forth, he gave a loud neigh that resounded through the glen. All the horses stopped what they were doing and turned to look at us.

"'Bout time we stopped," said Colby, panting away, coming up behind me. He rested his hands on his knees.

"*Shhh*," said Glooscap, over his shoulder. "You will scare them."

The others reached the top of the ridge, clustering behind us. No one spoke. The horses stared at us as if we'd intruded on their private gathering. They all remained motionless, their eyes wide, ears pointed, tails no longer swishing. Nervous.

Glooscap slipped the bundle from his shoulder and handed it to Brodan, then he began to cautiously inch toward the big black stallion, who I assumed was the leader of the herd. The other horses watched Glooscap intently as he approached. Inch by inch, Glooscap treaded forward, until he was only a few feet away. The stallion snorted and tossed his head, his black mane fluttering like a cape. When he was within a few feet, Glooscap began humming softly, reminding me of what I'd learned to do to soothe animals at Whispering Cedars.

When Glooscap was an arm's length away, he slowly lifted his hand. The stallion nudged it with his muzzle. The other horses wandered over to investigate the visitor, first surrounding Glooscap, then thrusting their noses toward him, as if they were trying to get a better sense of who had entered their sanctuary. Because it was a sanctuary with everything a horse could ever want—fresh water, plenty of grazing, trees for shelter and windbreak, and even soft bedding. It was more inviting than the spot we rested the night before on the banks of Cootamain, even more than the Sawnay village and longhouse where we'd slept. But then I preferred the freedom of the outdoors over the confines of walls. Walls made me feel claustrophobic, like the world might begin to close in and crush me, like I felt in those holding cells at court, and in my room at the youth detention.

At Whispering Cedars, on weekends during the warmer months, I'd head up into Montana's high country on horseback with old ranch hand Jerry and his son Rufus. We'd round up the ranch's cattle for a head count, checking to find out if any had fallen prey to mountain lions or grizzlies or wolves, or maybe broken a leg or fell over a cliff edge. It was during those times that I learned to love the night sky for its beauty and mystery, far away from the ranch's lights, far away from any artificial lights, under the cloak of night. The only lights were the waxing moon and glittering stars. The only sounds were the coyotes serenading the rolling black hills and the creatures that called them home, like a long lullaby that I never ever wanted to end, a lullaby that I'd fallen asleep to more times than I could count.

The longer I was away from it all, the more I missed it, the more I wanted to return, be with the land, be with the animals. Now I was there, sort of, only on a different world, with different people, different circumstances. And it felt good, all things considered.

After a few minutes, Glooscap motioned for me to come forward, I walked slowly on the balls of my feet to the horses. I lifted my hand up and a mare, chestnut with white patches, stepped away from the others. She moseyed over to me and began to sniff my palm tentatively. Then she whinnied loudly, took a few steps back, sending waves of skittishness through the herd.

Glooscap began to hum again, louder this time. He gestured for me to try again.

I reached out and rested my palm on the mare's muzzle. She shut her eyes. With my other hand, I rubbed her neck in long, gentle sweeping motions, causing a shiver to run through her body, and mine too.

As Glooscap continued to hum, he motioned the others forward. Slowly and silently, they inched into the glen and approached the herd. The horses surrounding Glooscap and I began to disperse. First, one young tan stallion with patches of white trotted proudly over to Simon, then a white-and-black mare to Anna. Within a minute, all of us were paired up, stroking a horse or resting a hand on some part of their bodies. Except for Colby, who was hanging back and bouncing from one foot to another, squirming like his feet were on fire. "I need to pee something fierce," he said, and took off behind a tree.

"He has the bladder of a child," said Cawop.

"Now, we ride north," said Glooscap. With that, he grasped the stallion's mane. He spryly leapt atop his back, then spun him three-sixty. The horse neighed and hoofed the earth. In my mare's large black eye, I could see my reflection. I clutched her mane and swung my leg up and over her back, her front quarters solid against my inner thighs. The others began to mount the horses that they'd chosen or—maybe a better way to put it—the horses that'd chosen them. They were all fine, healthy, powerful animals. Perfect specimens, as Vince would've said.

"Hey, I know you all trying to leave me behind," said Colby, emerging from some bushes.

"If we could only be so lucky," said Tabby, rolling her eyes.

A young stallion, tan with white patches, whinnied and trotted straight toward Colby, swooshing his tail side to side.

"Oh, yeah, that's a fine-looking ride," said Colby, giving his toothy smile. He waited until the stallion stopped next to him, and then he swung his leg over its back and leapt on.

"And to think you didn't have to steal it," said Tabby. "Bravo."

"Me and this guy got an understanding. Ain't that right?" said Colby as he petted the stallion's neck.

Suddenly, the stallion bucked once, then twice, almost sending Colby flying. He leaned forward, a panicked look on his face, and he quickly started petting his neck again, hoping to calm his mount.

Anna put her hand to her mouth, trying to catch her laughter before it spilled out, but she only managed to alter it to a snort.

"Hey, why are they called thunder horses?" said Simon, rubbing his stallion's forehead.

Glooscap and Brodan smiled mischievously at each other. "You will see if they choose to show you," said Glooscap. He then looked at each member of the group, nodding his head as if he was proud of us for managing so far. Then he spun his mount around and set his stallion trotting across the glen. I clicked my mouth and gave a hip thrust. My mare cantered after his stallion. Behind me, the others got into line. The remaining horses parted to allow us through, letting out a chorus of neighs that carried on well after we all left the glen.

27

Over the next few hours we rode silently, becoming acquainted with our mounts. There were no mishaps. Everyone managed to ride bareback better than I'd thought, even Colby. I was surprised at how quickly trust had formed between us and our mounts, as if we'd all been riding together for years.

It wasn't much different from riding in Montana. Sure, the trees were bigger, a lot bigger. And there were strange creatures, those three-ringed planets, and all sorts of other weird things I was sure we'd yet to encounter, but simply the feeling of riding was the same.

I hadn't realized how much I missed it. I'd ridden at Halton House a few dozen times. But it was always short rides, half hour, hour tops. Not like this, in the middle of nowhere with no civilization forever. Forever, forever. I rolled the word around in my mouth a few times. It sounded vast, endless, and infinite. Maybe this planet was larger than Earth, maybe a hundred times larger or maybe even a thousand. I didn't know, maybe no one did.

When we arrived at a fork in the trail, Glooscap stopped his stallion and got off. He looked down the trail to the right and then the one to the left, as if he was debating on which way to take.

"One is shorter, but rougher, not as safe," he said.

"What do you figure?" I said, and twisted back to look at the others.

Colby, Anna, and Tabby were already slouched over, worn out from the afternoon's ride. I didn't think they could handle another few hours, let alone a few hours of rough riding. Glooscap must've sensed this too, because without another word, he mounted his stallion and started off on the right trail. The one that was supposed to be safer.

28

Dejunga leads his braves along the river path past the Sawnay village, heading deeper into the skytrees. He and his braves move swiftly, their moccasins making them as silent as ghosts as they tread over the forest floor.

When he hears a voice, he stops his braves with a hand signal. They all crouch down in the undergrowth to hide. A second voice joins the first, and then footsteps. Two Sawnay boys walk toward them carrying baskets. Dejunga waits until they are near, and then he leaps onto the path. The boys drop their baskets and turn to flee. Dejunga slides his tomahawk from his belt, flips it once in his hand, and then throws the weapon. It spins through the air before striking one boy in the back. He drops to the ground face first to lay still. The other one stops and kneels down to help his friend. For his loyalty, he is swarmed by the Wendo braves. Before he can make a sound, they hack and cut him until he is no more.

"Give their spirits to our brother the wolf," says Dejunga as he steps over the bodies, leaving the braves to drag them into the undergrowth.

He does not want to come across any more Sawnay and alert them that a Wendo hunting party is passing through their territory. So, he stays farther from the path. All is quiet and uneventful. They do not come across anyone as they run like a pack of wolves through the skytrees.

Come late day, they arrive at the home of the thunder horses. When they begin to pass through, the horses erupt in fright and run to the far end of the clearing and do not stop making sounds until the Wendo have left. They continue to follow the path, leaving Sawnay territory far behind. At dusk, they arrive at a fork, where Hulaka kneels down and studies the tracks. "Eight horses went right," he says. "One horse went left later in the day."

"The Boy with the Scar is the only one who matters, for One Who Sees All," says Dejunga. "What path did the boy travel on?" Dejunga unties one of the shrunken totem heads from his belt and holds it at arm's length by its long black hair. He will ask the head and the head will tell him. He tilts back to fix on the tiny distant flicker of Mother Earth's sun in the darkening sky. He starts to chant deeply from his chest and dance around in a circle, the cycle of seasons, the cycle of life and death. His chanting grows louder, a song that Ragaroo had taught him. A song to reach into the Spirit World for guidance from the ones who have gone on before but who are not forgotten. He dances in a circle, chanting for some time. When he stops, he rolls the head toward the split in the path. It thuds and bounces and comes to rest facing right.

"The boy travels that way," says Dejunga, and nods in the direction the head faces.

They will stalk them and wait until the early hours before they attack. They will capture the boy and kill the others, on whose hearts they will feast. They are now too far from Wenda to bring back more prisoners.

Dejunga grins for the third time since they began their hunt. And among the Wendo, Dejunga is not known as man who grins.

29

The thunder horses took the trail with ease, as if they knew it as well as the trails I knew around Whispering Cedars. No one spoke as we rode into the early evening's violet sky.

Although I'd ridden bareback, it was never without reins. I found the mane worked pretty much the same. Little tug here, little tug there. No different really, only horse hair in my right hand instead of worn leather.

Glooscap glanced back once in a while, as he'd been doing when we were on foot, like a shepherd checking his flock. I found myself doing the same. It wasn't until the violet sky changed to purple and the air cooled a few more degrees that we arrived at a small clearing next to the trail, like a campsite. In the center, there was a firepit with charred remains.

"Are we going to stop?" said Anna, her voice tired. More locks had come undone, changing her last vestige of haughtiness to one of girl-next-door.

"We will spend the night here," said Glooscap, sliding from his stallion. "Leave at first light."

I got off my mare. I patted her flank a few times. "You did well," I said. "We both did." And with that, she whinnied and nudged my hand gently a few times.

"'Bout time we stopped," said Colby. "My ass aches."

"Wasn't as rough as I thought it would be," said Tabby.

After we all dismounted, the horses moseyed over to the edge of the clearing and began to munch on high green grass.

Brodan and Glooscap started collecting twigs and small branches for a fire. Simon and I dropped our bundles and cleaned out the charred remains from the firepit. The others all plunked down and began rooting through their bundles.

Within a few minutes, we amassed a large pile of firewood. Cawop built a small tepee of twigs in the firepit. Then he struck a piece of flint, shooting sparks against tattered strips of white bark. A small flame leapt to life. He blew on the flame until it grew. Then he added some of the larger twigs and the flames grew even higher. As the night darkened around us, the fire's glow pushed it back from the clearing, pushed it back from us.

It'd been a very long time, over a year, since I'd been out in the wilderness with horses and companions around a fire. There were so many times in the past, too many to count, where I'd been in a similar place, a comfortable place, where there were no distractions, like cellphones or video games or Internet or TV. These were places where all that you could hear were the natural sounds around you, the sounds people had been hearing since the dawn of humankind. I smiled sleepily, longingly. I sat there for a minute holding onto that smile. God, everything, all of it was beautiful right then.

The warm lick of flames echoed through that nature cathedral, the breeze shaping around those primeval trees, caressing my cheeks, playing that harpgrass somewhere in the night. I was in the present moment, like I couldn't ever remember being, totally amazed at that world I'd woken into the day before, which, sitting there like I was, thinking like I was, didn't seem all that different from Earth really.

Maybe it was me trying to come to terms with what had happened, to try to make things less frightening. Or maybe I was unwittingly preparing myself in case we didn't find a way home. In case we were stuck there, wherever there was.

I thought of the European explorers and the first time they stepped foot on the rugged coastline of the Pacific Northwest, with its snowcapped mountains and towering redwood cedars, and the native people they came across. They probably experienced that same initial shock and awe and wonder that we had. But then this was a different world, in a different solar system, not reached by sailing across an ocean. How did we end up here? I hadn't thought too hard on that question since we arrived, hadn't really had the chance to with the way we'd been constantly on the go making decisions. There'd been so much happening, so much to process every hour. There in that clearing as the fire warmed my face, I pondered. The Sawnay had come through some door, a stargate of sorts. Had our journey been a fluke? A one-in-a-billion event? Had we accidentally been sucked through some rift in time and space? I'd always heard of things like that happening. You know, planes and ships vanishing in the Bermuda Triangle. That type of thing. I heard about military planes and commercial passenger planes that seemed to vanish without a trace—there one minute, gone the next. But I never truly believed anything like that could really happen. I always assumed there had to be a reasonable explanation and that stuff was simply crank TV to watch on the History or Discovery channel, when nothing else was on. It was the stuff delusional quacks promoted, as old ranch hand Jerry would say. It was conspiracy theories, unexplained phenomena, events people tried to explain away with the fantastical. None of it had any bearing in the real world, where you could see, hear, touch, smell, and taste. The world I lived in. Yet, there we all were, a bunch of sleepy faces sitting around a fire on another world.

I tilted my head back, my breath wispy, and began to search for constellations that I knew I'd never find.

"Are you looking for Starpeople?" said Glooscap, sitting down beside me.

"Stars, not people," I said, a little confused. "What are Starpeople?"

"People who live among the stars and travel between them."

"Like UFOs? Flying saucers? Little gray men who abduct people?"

Glooscap smiled and laughed softly to himself.

"Hey, why did Poowasan call those three planets the Three Brothers?"

Glooscap poked the fire with a stick and watched an ember rise up in the night sky. "A long, long time ago, a Starwoman came to World of Dawn. She had three sons. She taught them the ways of the world. After she went back to the stars, her sons could not live in harmony with World of Dawn's other children. They were banished to the skies, to look over what they lost. Only when they learn to live in harmony can they return again. It is said they will be needed at this time."

I stared at the planets for a moment, then said, "Where's Cawop gone to?" He'd left a few minutes ago, hadn't returned.

"He watches," said Glooscap. "Brodan will go after, then me."

"Watching for what?" I said quietly.

"Man-eating beetles?" said Colby, piping in. "What else is out there? Thought the route was safe?" He plunked down between us.

"To watch is wise," said Glooscap, tossing the stick on the fire.

"What else is out there that you ain't telling us about?" said Colby.

Calmly Glooscap said, "There is a whole world out there." And then he got up and left like he didn't want to debate with Colby. For that, he was a good judge of character.

Anna stood up holding a black fur that she'd removed from her bundle. She held it out in front of her, as though she was trying to decide where to put it. She turned to me. "I've never slept outside without a tent before."

"Me neither," said Colby. "Park bench one time after a party. But that was downtown Detroit."

"I don't think any of us have, except maybe the bush boys," said Tabby. I knew she was referring to me and Simon; he had already stretched out on a fur beside me. Fact being, I'd slept outside more times than I could count, on the open grasslands of Montana, up in the rocky high country. I'd experienced it all, embracing every second of it from the very first time to that moment. I'd felt the calm and freedom and serenity of knowing there was so much more to life than the majority of people in the civilized world were led to believe. So much more.

I looked around at my companions. Some I'd known for months, others for only days. But I felt close to all of them right then. I dragged my bundle in front of me, untied the hide thongs, reached inside, and took out some of the dried meat. I passed a piece to Simon, then placed my bundle behind me and leaned back, chewing a strip of meat that tasted as scrumptious as steak. And to think, I could've been stuck eating a giant man-eating beetle with the innocent—yet somewhat appetizing—name of doda. But then maybe it wouldn't have been so bad, and right then I promised myself, if the opportunity arose again, I'd try it out, no questions asked.

A hand landed on my shoulder, Anna's hand. She used me for support as she sat down beside me. "What were you humming?" she said.

"Humming? I was humming?"

"Yeah, humming a song?"

I hadn't even been paying attention, but I knew what song. "A song my dad and I used to listen to."

"What song?"

"It's classic rock, from way back."

"He's dead?"

"Who?"

"Your dad?"

"Don't know . . . why do you ask?"

"Because you never talk about him. Just like my uncle doesn't talk about my Aunty Win."

"I guess because he's been gone such a long time."

"Do you think he'll come back?"

"I don't know, don't know if he's dead or maybe lives someplace else—maybe with a new family."

"That sucks," she said. "Maybe you'll find out one day."

"What happened to your Aunty Win?"

"You don't know?"

"That's why I'm asking."

"She was killed . . . well . . . murdered while my uncle was in Iraq. I can't believe you don't know the story. That's why he opened Halton House. That's why he does what he does."

"You don't talk about some things either," I said, making a conscious effort not to look at her stomach.

"Like what?"

She eyed me suspiciously, and said, "Like what things?"

I didn't reply.

"Like what? Tell me what you mean!"

"Forget it," I said, and turned away. I didn't think it was the time or place to mention the text messages that I'd read on the bluff.

She waved her hands about dramatically. "What? Is it none of your—not the *time* or *place*?"

"It's nothing," I said, wishing I hadn't hinted at anything.

We both sat there silently for a minute, as if we both knew she'd gone a little too far, and then she got up. "Good night, Tanner."

"Hey, I would've carried your purse," I said.

"You never offered to—Brodan did," she said. She went to leave, but stopped. "Thank you."

"For what?" I said.

"The river," she said, then she bent over to peck me quickly on the lips. I could smell perfume faintly on her, even after all we'd been through. "We're old souls, you and I," she said, then rounded the fire to rejoin her sister, leaving me baffled, wondering what the heck had just happened, trying to remember when I last kissed a girl.

I caught a flash in my periphery. A green light streaked across the dark sky. I watched what I thought was a shooting star, until it came to a dead stop. It paused there a moment, then it changed course and streaked in the other direction to become lost among the billions of stars. Gone in a flash. Then, without a sound, Glooscap sat down cross-legged.

"Did you see that?" I said.

"See what?" he said, tossing a stick on the fire.

Pointing to where I'd last seen the light, I said, "That green light."

"Starpeople."

"You're pulling my chain."

"Pulling your chain?"

"Yeah, you know, you're joking around," I said.

"I don't joke about Starpeople," he said, deadpan.

I gazed up at the sky again in wonder.

"If we leave at first light, we will reach Ambrose's by nightfall."

"It'll be a long day," I said. "Hard on the others."

Glooscap glanced around the fire. "Hard on Colby and Anna. They do not like horses."

Colby had lain down on his side, with his back to the fire, his eyes closed.

"They don't ride a lot of horses in Detroit or San Francisco," I said.

"De-troit?"

"A city in the state of Michigan."

"Ah, cities—San Francisco, Washington, New York."

"Yeah, cities like those. Hang on a sec, how do you know about San Francisco, Washington, and New York, but not Detroit?"

Glooscap shrugged his shoulders. "Ambrose taught the Sawnay much about the United States of America. Many Sawnay know the names of all states and cities. Ambrose gifted Poowasan and the elders with maps made by white men."

"So, Ambrose must be from the United States?" I said. "Why do the Sawnay bother to learn anything about Earth? I mean, if you're never going back, that is."

Glooscap was silent for a second, as if he was putting a lot of thought into his answer, and then said, "The Sawnay know it is important to be prepared."

"I guess that's smart."

"Have you ridden on a steam locomotive?" he said.

"Locomotive? Not one of those, but a subway," I said. "Pretty much the same thing."

Glooscap tossed a few sticks onto the fire. "Mother Earth is a very strange place now."

I chuckled softly. "You should watch a Lady Gaga video on MTV."

"Lady Gaga?"

"She's a performer. MTV is music television. It plays music videos by artists—bands, singers, rap groups, that sort of stuff. You watch a screen and see images of people and hear songs . . . and don't even get me started on YouTube."

"Songs, as you heard in the longhouse?"

"Kinda, but different. The performers record their songs so they can be replayed. People can see them over and over again." That was the best I could do to explain it right then, the way sleep was clawing at my mind. Besides, it was a conversation that could've went on for hours, a conversation which would probably never happen, I thought, because sometime over the next few days, we'd be going our separate ways. The Sawnay would head north, and we would head home to Earth. Hopefully. "How many of these stargates exist?"

"I am unsure. My people left our land in what is now called California, to travel south into Mexico. That is where we traveled from."

The talk around the fire had died down. Anna and Tabby were walking over to some bushes at the edge of the clearing, headed to the washroom. I was about to call out and ask if they wanted me to go with them, but they looked like they were fine without a chaperone.

"Good night, Tanner," said Glooscap. With that, he stood and rounded the fire to sit beside Brodan, Cawop still nowhere in sight. I took the fur out of my bundle and unfurled it on the ground beside Simon, far enough away from the fire so that I wouldn't get burned by any stray embers. Other questions I had would have to wait.

"Did my eyes deceive me or did I just see Anna kiss you a few minutes ago?"

"Your eyes deceived you," I said, and then changed the subject. "They have maps. Know about the U.S. and Canada, locomotives, names of cities. They said Ambrose taught them. But why wouldn't he teach about cars or TVs or airplanes?"

"Maybe he didn't think those were important," said Simon, shrugging. "He actually said locomotives?"

I nodded and lay back. "Doesn't make sense to me."

"Maybe Ambrose is Amish or Mennonite."

"I don't know—it's odd."

"Yeah, but then everything about this place is odd," he said, and yawned. "I swear I saw Cawop talking to a raven earlier when we stopped."

"I think I saw a UFO."

He chuckled, and said, "You're tired, that's all."

"What if we could help the Sawnay? I mean, what if we could make a difference here. Balance out the scales for all the bad we did, for what we did back home."

"Wowowo—balance the scales?" he whispered harshly, leaning into me.

"Yeah, balance the scales."

"Are you gonzo? Where's this coming from, man? We almost died twice—and we promised Conroy we'd go home the first chance we get. Remember? Look, if something happens, we can't call 911. If we get into trouble, there's no cavalry coming to our rescue. That's it, we're done."

"I'm just thinking that maybe this would be a way to . . . I don't know . . . make things right."

"Don't start preaching—please don't start preaching," he said.

"They could use our help."

"Okay, let's just say I was to say *yes*, which I'm not saying, but let's just say." He tossed his chin to Anna and Tabby who had just emerged from the bushes. "Are you willing to risk their lives for some romantic idea of . . . being a hero?"

When I didn't reply, he quickly rolled onto his side so his back was toward me and pulled the fur over his body.

"Simon."

He turned his head slightly to better hear me. "Yeah."

"Good night, Simon."

"Good night."

I nestled my head into my bundle. In the distance, wolves were howling. The Three Brothers shone brightly. The stars glittered dazzlingly like jewels, and I tried to recall if I'd ever seen them in such a way. As I counted them, I found myself imagining that there was someone on one of those planets counting me right then.

I only reached twenty-two, before my eyes shut.

30

In the dead of night, Dejunga hides in the shadows beside the trail like a Windigo waits to take a man's spirit. His face and body are covered in black soot and he holds a vulture wing at his side. A gift for the Sawnay traitor. He is there for only a short while, when the sound of hooves thudding on the path alerts him that the traitor approaches. Cawop rides erect and vigilant of the surrounding forest. Dejunga has been stalking along the Shadow Road for many moons, and so now he is one with the shadows. So Cawop does not see him until he steps out onto the trail directly in front of the thunder horse.

Whinnying, it steps back, kicks its front hooves into the air, kicks at the shadows as if to scare them away. But Dejunga knows shadows do not scare away. A raven flies up into the canopy. He cannot remember seeing a raven fly at night.

"Where are the others?" says Dejunga.

"Sleeping. Soon forever."

"And you will be new chief of the Sawnay," says Dejunga.

"And take Poowasan's daughters as my lifegivers."

"Ragaroo has promised everything you hunger for," says Dejunga. He hands the vulture wing to Cawop, who holds it up in the starlight and runs his fingers over the feathers.

"Who is following the party?" says Dejunga.

"No one," says Cawop. "Only we left the village."

Dejunga shakes his head. "Another thunder horse follows you. The rider went left at the fork."

"A lonely horse," says Cawop, shrugging.

There is a flash in the night from a peculiar-looking bundle that the traitor carries. Then Dejunga notices strange white moccasins on his feet. "Who made the bundle?"

Cawop lifts the bundle at his side, looks at it. "A man named Gucci from Mother Earth."

"And the moccasins?" says Dejunga.

Cawop kicks his feet out and smiles like a fox. "I took them from one of the boys. The one whose skin is all black. A man named Nike made them."

"Powerful medicine," says Dejunga, nodding approvingly.

"Very powerful medicine."

"Black Skin owned the bundle too?"

"No, a girl."

Dejunga opens the pouch on his hip. He takes out the shine box and touches the front until the lighted picture appears. He shows the pale-skin Yankee girl to Cawop. "This girl?"

"That is her—Anna from Earth. Her sister also travels with them."

Dejunga nods, a thrill coursing through him. Two head totems are always better than one.

Cawop starts to move on, but stops and says, "Glooscap is with them."

"I know," he says, and he lifts his right hand, which is missing three fingers. "He owes me his spirit, and his spirit I will take."

Then Cawop smiles and urges the horse forward on the trail and leaves him behind. Dejunga stands there for a while, watching Cawop leave. The only thing Dejunga hates more than a traitor is a thief, especially one whose voice sounds like a dog giving life to puppies. If you want to take from someone, you take their spirit first, as Dejunga will take Glooscap's. And then Cawop's when the

Wendo attack the village of the Sawnay. He will then feast on his heart and take the bundle made by the man named Gucci, and the white moccasins by the man Nike. Then, he will take Poowasan's daughters for himself.

As he slips back into the shadows, he hears wings flapping overhead. The raven flies after Cawop. And Dejunga is certain he has never seen a raven at night. He starts off to return to where his braves are preparing for battle, his ghost moccasins treading silently over the forest floor.

And for the fourth time since he came down from his mountain village, Dejunga grins. And among the Wendo, Dejunga is not known as man who grins.

31

I awoke to a hot sensation on my chest, sometime during that magic time when night mingles with day, just before sunrise. I lay there unmoving and listening to the sing-song of birds high in the trees. All the horses were awake and clustered together, wide-eyed, neighing nervously, except one. The mare Cawop had been riding was gone.

"Tanner, Tanner," said a hushed voice in my ear. It startled me because I hadn't heard anyone approach. Glooscap was kneeling at my side, leaning in closely, as he'd done in the longhouse the previous morning.

"Where's Cawop? And what's going on with the horses?" I said, propping up on my elbows, blinking sleep from my eyes. He motioned with his hands for me to be quiet. There was a dull ache in my body from the previous day's hard riding. And with this ache, I knew the others would be sore, much sorer than me.

"There is something coming," said Glooscap.

"What is it?" I said, my heart picking up.

He didn't respond, his fierce eyes were fixed on the forest back in the direction from which we'd come. "We must wake the others and go," he said urgently.

He stood up suddenly and headed over to Brodan who was still sleeping. He knelt down and spoke words in Sawnay. I looked around—Simon, Colby, the girls, but no Cawop. There was no empty fur, no sign that he'd ever been there. I rolled onto my side, got to my feet, and went over to Anna and Tabby who were still asleep beside each other under a fur, Tabby holding Anna.

"Get up," I said, shaking Anna's shoulder. "We need to leave."

Tabby opened her eyes first. She gave me a groggy, confused look, as if she'd been expecting to wake up someplace much different, maybe back home in San Francisco or Halton House or somewhere else on Earth.

"Come on," I said. "We need to move." She smiled dreamily like she thought I was playing some kind of joke on her, the kind we played almost daily back at Halton House. But then she focused on me, sensing there was something else going on.

"Now, Tabby. Get Anna up too." Her eyes popped open. "Get up, get up, we're leaving." When I was certain that she fully understood the urgency, I rushed over to Colby who was sleeping on his side with a folded T-shirt shrouding his eyes, like all the youths did in the detention center to block the nightlight's yellow glow. I jostled his shoulder, hoping to wake him quicker than I did Tabby, hoping he wouldn't be typical Colby and try to argue with me.

"Hey, man," he said, lifting his head. "I'm taking me another hour. My ass aches and my spine's all rattled up."

"We need to leave, lickety-split," I said.

"Whatcha talking 'bout, man? Wake me up for breakfast, after that fire's nice and toasty," he said, and rolled back onto his side. Please, not now, I thought.

I grabbed his arm and tugged him back. He clutched my hand and pulled off his blind. "Touch me again. Something's going to happen to you, all right."

"This isn't a joke," I said, the pouch's heat increasing on my chest. "If you don't get up . . ."

Colby looked at Anna and Tabby as they hurriedly shoved furs into their bundles. Someone had awoken Simon. He was packing his bundle, too. Colby released my hand and nodded as though he finally got it. He threw off his fur and sprang to his feet. He started searching the ground around his bundle, becoming frantic, and said, "My shoes, my shoes are gone—someone stole my shoes!"

"Forget the shoes," I said, sensing a change in the forest.

"You crazy, man. Those cost three hundred bucks," he said. "My socks gone too—what am I supposed to wear on my feet?"

"Just hurry," I said, and hustled back over to where I'd been sleeping to roll up my fur. The horses were casting glances back down the trail, their eyes wide and legs restless. I'd seen horses act that way when a predator—wolf, bear, or mountain lion—was too close for comfort, their scent in the air. I stuffed my fur into my bundle, tied the thongs off, and slung it over my shoulder.

Glooscap and Brodan had notched arrows in their bows. An early amber sunrise scintillated down through the canopy, lighting up areas of the forest and leaving others inky dark. Then a fleeting movement, something shadowy between two trees, caught my attention. I watched for it again, waiting, my heart quickening.

A whizzing sound broke the magic-time silence. A spear struck the ground mere inches from my feet, quivering back and forth. Someone let out a blood-curdling scream. I whirled around. Brodan tottered back and forth, a spear protruding from his gut. Then he stumbled forward and collapsed onto his side, clutching the spear shaft.

Anna shrieked, covering her face with both hands. Tabby grabbed her shoulders and pulled her toward the thunder horses. They were neighing and jostling into one another.

Colby and Simon had their bundles shouldered, crouching near the firepit, glancing around, panic-stricken, unsure what to do.

"Follow the trail," yelled Glooscap, drawing his bow. "I'll find you." Then he let fly an arrow. I knew he wouldn't run. I knew he would stay and fight whoever the attackers were, whoever had speared Brodan. I stepped over to the spear that'd missed me by inches. I yanked it from the earth. I hefted it in my hands, light, balanced, about six feet long—just like the javelins I'd used in gym class, only the tip of it was obsidian instead of steel.

Simon and Colby rushed toward their horses. Anna had already mounted her mare, but Tabby's mare was riderless and she was nowhere in sight.

A loud horn blared deafeningly, filling the early dawn, causing a shudder to run through my body. Shadows separated from shadows. They moved toward us like things from a nightmare, wielding weapons. I reached my arm back. I aimed at the one directly in front of me and hurled the spear at the same time Glooscap's bowstring pinged.

The spear vanished into the cloak of shadow. A savage howl filled the night, as if a mortal wound had been dealt. It hit the ground, and began writhing and convulsing. There was a commotion behind me. Colby and Simon were wrestling someone to the ground. Another shadow leapt over the one I'd dropped, coming straight at me, whirling a tomahawk above its head.

"Go now," screamed Glooscap. He tossed his head toward the horses as he drew back another arrow. He wanted me to flee with the others, but I wouldn't abandon him and leave him to fight on his own—I couldn't.

Another shadow darted from the forest, turning into a man in the early sunrise, bare-chested and wiry, his face painted black, body streaked like tiger stripes. When he reached an opening, I saw that he was actually bald, except for a black rooster of hair on the top of his head. He carried two long obsidian knives and moved eerily silently toward Brodan, almost like a ghost over the ground. I looked around for something to use as a weapon. Then I remembered Conroy's Swiss Army knife in the kangaroo pouch on my shirt. Hastily, I pulled out the knife and opened the small blade just as Rooster Hair arrived at Brodan and bent over him. I took a final look back. Simon and Colby were on their horses galloping north on the trail.

I ran at Rooster Hair, the small blade in my hand glaringly inadequate. "Hey—get away from him," I yelled.

Rooster Hair turned to me and all I saw were the whites of his eyes, teeth that had been sharpened, which made me think of shark teeth. He snatched Brodan's hair and jerked his head back. Brodan tried feebly to grab his attacker's hands, crying out in pain. Grinning maniacally, Rooster Hair plunged an obsidian knife deep into Brodan. His hands instantly flopped to the ground, his life extinguished like a blown-out candle. Then I noticed something on Rooster Hair's hip. Instead of pouches tied to his belt like Glixtan's, there were two darkened, shriveled heads, unmistakable with their mouths agape in silent, endless screams.

He roared like a beast as he wrenched his obsidian knife free, and plunged it again and again into Brodan's lifeless body. Then he threw Brodan face down. Out of the corner of my eye, I saw something flying toward me. Another spear whizzed by my head. Two more shadows emerged from the forest, heading straight for me. Then a spear soared between the two shadows. Someone had thrown it from behind me.

I turned around. It was Tabby, looking on as if she wanted to stay with us and fight.

"Get out of here," I screamed. "You're gonna get killed."

She stood her ground, unmoving.

"Now—go," I screamed.

She hesitated a moment, then dashed to her mare, mounted, and urged the horse north after the others.

"You go too, Tanner," said Glooscap, backing up. I took a final look at the scene.

"But Brodan?"

"It is too late," he said, drawing his bow.

Brodan's lifeless body lay sprawled out on the ground, Rooster Hair standing overtop, the black paint on his face streaking from sweat. He saw me, then he placed his obsidian knife to his mouth and began to lick the blade clean. Then he rushed at me.

He moved with inhuman speed, more like a wild animal. His hand shot out to snatch one of Glooscap's arrows in midair. Without missing a step, he came on. He wasn't so lucky with the second arrow. It hit him in the shoulder. The third arrow he dodged by rolling backward. Then he sprung to his feet and dove into the bushes.

Glooscap was right. It was too late. As I ran to my mare, I folded up the tiny Swiss Army knife. I leapt on. She spun around. She trotted ten strides, then burst into a full gallop after Tabby and the others. She moved without guidance. She took the trail like she knew it well, around protruding rocks and tangles of tree roots, up the steeper sections, navigating the snaky turns, huffing and grunting, her ears pinned against her head, her muscles contracting as I urged her onward. It was as if she knew we needed to get as far away from what had happened as quickly as possible. And so we did.

32

The faster we went, the more I hunched against my mare's body, my chest against her neck, my knees tight against her flexing front quarters. I stole a glance back. Glooscap was coming up behind me, his big stallion's head pumping back and forth as if it was helping him build momentum. Brodan's riderless mare ran alongside.

As I rounded a bend on the trail, Simon came into view ahead of me. He was off to the side, looking back over his shoulder through a fall of white blooms drifting in the breeze, millions of them in the morning light. When he realized that I wasn't slowing down, he urged his stallion forward. I reached him and we both raced along the trail, side by side, Glooscap closing the distance behind us. Suddenly I felt a feeling of weightlessness, and the thunder horse, my mare, lifted off the ground. I glanced down to make sure I wasn't mistaken, and sure enough we were two, maybe three feet off the ground, galloping on nothing but air. I turned back. Glooscap's stallion was also airborne, only a few horse lengths behind me. It felt like there was a shift in time, and we were moving faster.

We rounded a curve and the others were there—Colby, Anna, and Tabby—on the trail. They were in a cluster looking back, unsure whether they should keep going or wait for the rest of us to catch up. I waved them onward. They took off and started riding hard, and in moments they all too were off the ground, all moving at breakneck speed. And there were no sounds of hooves, no ground rumbling underneath, only huffing and panting, and boughs brushing against boughs as the breeze from our Pegasus-like flight buffeted them.

My body was shaky from the adrenaline coursing through it. I'd been in enough tussles over the years—since my father left, since bouncing around from town to town—to know that feeling, or as old ranch hand Jerry liked to say, "When the primitive man awakens."

My thoughts raced. We'd faced a band of attackers, and one of whom killed Brodan right in front of my eyes, another almost killing me. And I might've actually killed someone too, with my own two hands. I'd thrown that spear in self-defense, not sure of the outcome, not sure if I would actually hit the shadowy figure that I knew was a man, flesh and bone. I couldn't recall taking aim, but I must have. Otherwise, I was certain right then that I would've been dead, laying back there on the trail with a spear sticking out of my belly, or my head caved in, or maybe a hole in my heart from one of Rooster Hair's obsidian knives.

Taking a deep breath, I tried to slow down my racing thoughts.

I don't know how long we rode for, our two groups separated by a few horse lengths. Eventually, the thunder horses all began to slowly descend, as though they sensed we were no longer in danger. A similar shift in time happened, only now we slowed down. We had ridden them hard, so hard that by the time we stopped, they were completely lathered in sweat. Everyone was out of breath, horses and riders. Anna looked the worst, her complexion waxy, and all the blood drained from her face. Both Simon and Colby's eyes were wild-looking. They nervously scanned the surrounding forest, like they expected something bad to happen at any moment.

After everyone had a minute to catch their breath, Tabby said, "What just happened?" Her voice was shaky.

No one spoke up. Glooscap was looking back down the trail.

"Is he dead?" said Anna, sniffling. Her face was streaked with tears. "Brodan, is he dead?"

I was sure they'd seen Brodan hit by the spear, but not finished off by Rooster Hair. I wondered if any of them had ever seen someone murdered before, or even seen a dead person.

"I couldn't stop it," I said, and turned away, feeling waves of guilt wash over me.

"No one could have," said Glooscap.

"This isn't supposed to be happening," said Anna. She began to shake her head. "They said it was safe, the journey to see Ambrose." She looked from face to face as if she hoped someone would agree with her. "It's supposed to be safe, right?"

"No guarantees any place safe," said Colby in almost a whisper. "Better believe that—life's cheap in some neighborhoods." He was barefoot. Obviously, he hadn't found his shoes. "All I know is that asshole we tangled with will be drinking through a straw for the next eight weeks." He fist-bumped Simon. "He smelled rank like a city dumpster on a hot day. Man, he's a nasty bastard."

"No, he smelled like rotten meat," said Simon.

"Maybe they mistook us for someone else?" said Tabby. "That could be it, right?"

"That's stupid, and you know it," said Simon.

"They were Wendo braves, stalkers, led by Dejunga," said Glooscap. "They never journey this far north unless . . ."

"Unless, what, man? Come on, finish whatcha you gonna say." said Colby.

"Unless hunting for something . . . or someone," said Glooscap.

Colby scoffed, shaking his head. "I knew it wasn't right—from the beginning. I knew something messed up was gonna happen. And here we are. Everything's all messed up."

"Look," I said, "we might've gotten far enough away, but let's not take any chances. Let's keep riding."

Everyone was silent.

"Are you all right?" said Anna.

"I'm fine," I said, and gave my mare a pat on the neck.

The horses were still skittish. Glooscap looked from person to person, double-checking to ensure everyone was okay. Then he focused on me.

"Never do that again," he said, almost yelling. "You listen to me. You go when I tell you to go." Even in the early dawn light, I could make out sweat running down his face. He seemed unsure of what to do next. We were so awash with emotion from the initial attack that the shock of the thunder horses leaving the ground seemed insignificant. No one even mentioned it.

"Come on, guys, let's go," I said.

"How much farther to Ambrose's?" said Simon.

"We will reach it by nightfall," said Glooscap.

"What about Brodan?" said Anna, glancing back down the trail.

"Yeah, we can't just leave him back there," said Tabby.

Glooscap exhaled loudly. "If he is there when I return, I will take him home."

"If he's there? Why wouldn't he be there?" I said.

Glooscap shook his head and looked down at his stallion's mane, as if he didn't want to answer. "The Wendo . . . the Wendo do things."

"What kind of things?" said Anna, her voice high.

"Oh, nononono . . . nonono, no frigging way, man," said Colby. "I knew it—cannibals—I knew it!"

"What about Cawop?" said Simon. "Where's Cawop?"

"He did not return from his watch," said Glooscap.

"His mare was gone," I said. "He must've come back."

"My purse is gone," said Anna. Gucci was absent from her side. "Do you think he stole my purse? Why would he steal my purse?" I remembered the way Cawop had been fixated on her purse in the longhouse.

"That's just great," said Colby, kicking up his bare feet. "He came back to steal her purse, steal my shoes and socks, run off on his horse. Safe trip, no problems. Man, I'm sick of this place. Birds the size of airplanes, all sorts of crazy-ass bugs, people chucking spears, cannibal-ass motherfuckers. No saddles. And my balls ache like they've been hit with a sledgehammer—what's next?"

Suddenly, Colby's stallion reared up, kicking his front legs. Colby soared off his back and thudded to the ground, on his side, air blown from his lungs. Winded, he rolled onto his back gasping for air, clutching his chest.

I hissed through my teeth. It hurt. It hurt a lot, and I hadn't been the one dumped. I got off my mare and went to help him up.

"I don't need you—piss off," he groaned, and swatted my hand away, getting shakily to his feet. His eyes locked onto me, and he shook his head. "You all voted Windigo Road—betcha all regretting that now. Should've stayed in the city." He dusted off his backside, climbed onto his stallion, and nudged him forward to take the lead.

33

By mid-afternoon, the landscape began to change. There were fewer trees and they were farther apart, allowing more light to reach the forest floor. Lush, verdant plants abounded, bushy yellow flowers with crimson petals. Colorful birds like hummingbirds, only the size of seagulls, flitted around the flowers, pausing overtop just long enough to draw nectar with their stiletto beaks. All of it would've seemed beautiful, I thought, if what'd happened hours ago hadn't really happened, if it'd been a dream, or a nightmare, and not a reality. But no matter how hard I tried to see the beauty around me, it wouldn't appear. It was as if my perceptions had been smeared by violence and death.

It didn't take long before sweat was running down my face, stinging my eyes. The friction of my thighs against my mare had worked up a good lather. Glooscap was the only one of us who still rode erect, remaining vigilant of our surroundings. The rest of us rode like jellyfish that'd been concussed by dynamite, our limp faces and bodies conveying the horror we'd experienced, the loss of one companion, and the possible betrayal of another.

I rode up beside Glooscap. "We need to stop, just for a while."

"We will arrive at Ambrose's before nightfall," he said, like he really didn't want to stop.

"I know, you keep saying that. But look, I don't think they'll make it," I said. "Unless we rest."

He looked back at the others as if he was trying to gauge for himself whether or not we should rest. It was like he'd been so vigilant since the attack that he'd failed to notice how worn-out the rest of the group had become. That irked me greatly, and I had to bite my tongue. Just as I was about to remind him again that they didn't have a whole lot of saddle time—let alone riding without one—he pulled his stallion to a stop.

"We will get off the horses here," he said loud enough for the others to hear.

"Thank God," said Anna. "My back feels like it's broken."

"Finally, we gonna take a break," said Colby.

"No, no break, now we walk," said Glooscap. "We need to reach Ambrose's by night fall."

"Man, you a regular slave driver," said Colby, sucking his teeth for the first time in days. He lifted a bare foot. "And what am supposed to do 'bout my feet? I got no shoes because your boy robbed me."

"He's right to keep moving," said Simon, scanning our surroundings. "Another night out here isn't a good idea."

Everybody needed a break. My body was aching, and even the thunder horses were dragging their hooves. But Simon was right: that spending another night out in the forest wasn't smart. Our new circumstance called for shelter. Walking the horses wasn't nearly as good as taking a break, but it was better than carrying on on horseback. Being on our feet would give everyone's blood a chance to circulate through their legs again, help relieve tight and aching muscles, and reduce some back compression. One by one, we all came to a stop and dismounted. We all began walking on the trail in pairs, with our thunder horses beside us.

"This Dejunga, he the one that killed Brodan?" I said to Glooscap.

"Yes," he said.

"You think the Wendo are hunting for us?" I whispered.

"We will reach Ambrose's camp by nightfall if we do not stop," he said. "And we will be safe when we arrive."

"You've said that ten times. I get it. We need to keep moving—but why'd the Wendo attack us?"

"If we do not reach Ambrose's camp by nightfall, we might never reach it," he said. He said it in a way that made me believe him.

I grabbed his arm and said, "What did they want? Why'd they attack us? Horses? What was it?"

He jerked away from me, his big stallion neighed at his side. He was still hiding something from me, that much I was certain of. What it was, I didn't know.

"Is there something you're not telling me?" I said louder than I'd intended.

Anna and Tabby took notice.

"Come on, tell us," I said. "Go ahead, let's hear it."

"Yeah, tell us, man," said Colby.

"The Wendo were once friends of the Sawnay, but they lost their way. Their hate grew until it claimed their spirits."

"Hate for who?" said Anna.

"They were massacred by the white settlers' army, starved and forced to leave their lands. Almost all of their people died. Elders, lifegivers, children, babies."

"That's horrible," said Anna, hand to her mouth.

"Oh, that's just great, man. Crazy-ass cannibals with a hard-on for Americans," said Colby.

"This is getting worse and worse," said Simon, sighing. "Now, he wants vengeance on us?"

"Why us?" I said.

"I do not know," said Glooscap, and said no more. He turned and started walking away, and when I looked back everyone was staring at me, as if they were waiting for me to say more to him. But I didn't. I let things go at that. Not the right time or place.

As we carried on, the dull throb in my groin began to subside. My body loosened up as blood flowed throughout my legs. By the way the others were limping and hobbling, I could tell they were saddle-sore, or bareback sore—however you wanted to put it.

Two hours later, we finally stopped, sat down to eat a snack on the trail. No one talked much. We ate quickly, then began north again. The forest gradually opened up even more, changing to a swampy landscape—the Black Swamp. The air became humid. Dark stagnant pools stretched like long tendrils in every direction. On the surface rested giant green lily pads that I thought could've supported the weight of a human. Mushroom-shaped gray trees dotted the landscape, thick bluish moss hanging from their branches. Everywhere, bushy green ferns abounded, their leaves wrapped in purple vines. Occasionally, there'd be a loud splash in one of the pools. But when I looked, I could never find the cause.

Come early afternoon, my hide clothing was totally soaked in sweat. That made walking uncomfortable, or maybe trudging would be a better word. The pools got bigger, broken once in a while with a ripple here and there, caused by what, I couldn't say. And those pools became even bigger and farther-reaching the deeper we got into the swamp. A multi-colored dragonfly, the size of a remote control drone, landed on my mare's head, my reflection in its eyes a thousand-fold. When my mare gave a shake, the dragonfly took flight, its wings thrumming, to chase after a swarm of small flying insects.

Soon it was nightfall. Fog began to rise from the ground to hover thickly in the air, and my companions became gray figures, vague and spectral. As we rode on, I began to get drowsy from monotony. My eyes kept shutting. I'd open them, shake my head to try to clear the cobwebs, unsure how long they'd been closed for. No one talked. The only sounds were swamp critters singing.

When a scream erupted from somewhere behind us, I twisted around. All I could see was a wall of fog. Glooscap spun his stallion three-sixty.

"Follow the trail," he yelled, tossing his bundle to Colby, "and you will reach Ambrose's." Then he urged his stallion into a gallop, heading south toward the source of the scream, back the way we'd come. No sooner had he left than another scream tore through the swamp. I had no idea where he was going, but I wasn't prepared to let him go alone. I tossed my bundle to Simon, then chased after Glooscap into the fog, toward whatever dangers awaited

34

My mare galloped full-out through the thickening fog into the deepening darkness, her hooves swift over the ground. But she was tired, her stride and pace choppy. In the medicine pouch on my chest, the stones began generating heat again as they'd done on the two other occasions when danger had been near. Even though we weren't moving as fast as earlier, I was still afraid to let go of my mare's mane to take the hot pouch away from my skin, even for a second, even when it felt as if it was beginning to burn.

When Glooscap's stallion reared up and kicked its front legs, whinnying and chuffing wildly, I knew we'd arrived. Then I saw it through the fog. A writhing, black shape constricting a fallen horse. A snake. A massive snake. A momentary paralysis overcame my limbs, and I stood there taking it all in, fixed, frozen.

The fallen horse's eyes bulged as it chomped the air desperately, gasping for breath. Its legs were splayed at odd angles, kicking the air feebly. Two people—Channa and Maroona—stood on the far side of the snake, at the edge of the foggy dark. Beside them that mangy, one-eyed dog from the village was hunched low, barking crazily. I couldn't understand what they were doing there? And by themselves?

The snake's head rose up, its yellow eyes fixed on me. It was bigger than a fully grown python or anaconda, longer and thicker, like a fallen tree that'd come to life. It was the size of Titanoboa, the prehistoric snake I'd seen on a Discovery Channel documentary. Maybe it was Titanoboa. The head swayed back and forth menacingly a few times, then twisted and lunged at the girls. Chana thrust a spear in an attempt to keep it at bay, as Maroona held onto her.

"Tanner," said Glooscap. He tossed me a spear that he'd taken from the Wendo, leaping from his stallion. He hit the ground and drew his bow. As soon as my feet touched the ground, I rushed forward. Glooscap let fly an arrow, which hit the snake below its head, burying halfway to the red fletching. My body unfroze and I leapt to action.

But suddenly the back of my calves were swept out with a mighty blow that sent me careening. I landed on my hands and feet like a cat, heard a whoosh overhead and saw the snake's tail arcing through the air. My mare sidestepped quickly out of the way, just in time to avoid being struck.

Another arrow hit the snake. I charged forward, hoping to draw its attention away from the girls. It whirled around to face me, opening its maw to reveal two long fangs the size of hunting knives and hundreds of smaller razor-sharp teeth. Spittle drooled from its lower jaw.

I brought the spear back, then thrust it into the body below the head. The snake reeled, hissing, tearing the spear from my hands.

"Over here. Move, move," I yelled, waving Chana and Maroona onward.

Chana pulled Maroona along as the snake thrashed from side to side. It began uncoiling from the broken horse. Another arrow struck it, giving the girls a chance to dash to my side. I took Chana's spear, lunged forward to meet the snake head-on and stabbed its tough underbelly. It unleashed a hissing and thrashed about.

Out of the corner of my eye, I caught the tail cutting through the fog a second before it struck my shoulder and knocked me to the ground. A sharp pain shot through my arm, as if it had been struck by a sledgehammer. The dog darted between me and the snake, barking and growling, doing its best to be intimidating. Then I felt it begin to coil around my legs, tightening and crushing. I was stuck. The spear was too long—Conroy's Swiss Army knife! I pulled it from my kangaroo pouch, fumbling to flip out the blade, just as the snake's head came within striking distance. I stabbed its eye, burying the entire blade. It hissed and uncoiled from around my legs.

I scrambled to my feet. The snake retreated in large sweeping S motions, the protruding arrows making it look as if it'd been attacked by a porcupine. The girls were then behind me, holding onto each other, near their horse which had been mangled and crushed so severely that I couldn't discern whether it was a mare or stallion. Another arrow hit the snake as it retreated toward a pool.

A loud horn suddenly blared, the same horn I'd heard earlier that morning when we'd been attacked. Then three men—faces painted black, bare-chested—ran toward us screaming and wielding tomahawks. Leading them was Dejunga, a savage expression on his face. Then I saw it. Brodan's head was fastened to his hipbelt, bouncing around, joining the other two heads in their silent, endless screams.

Glooscap let an arrow fly. It hit one attacker in the chest and sent him rolling on the ground. Dejunga closed the distance between us swiftly. I had just enough time to defend myself with the spear raised overhead, a hand on each end, before he brought his tomahawk thundering down, vibrating the spear painfully in my hands. I pushed him back. He retreated a few steps. He swung his tomahawk in large loops as though he was searching for an opening. Then he lunged forward and took a powerful, well-aimed swing at my head. I ducked and thrust the spear. He gracefully sidestepped, whirled off to the right and then leapt forward again, shoulder first, crashing into me and sending both of us down to the soft ground. We both struggled to get on top of the other. Then he straddled me. He was all muscle, like corded steel. He clenched my throat with one hand and raised his tomahawk, preparing to deliver a fatal blow. Then he looked into my eyes, grinning the most wicked grin, revealing those shark teeth, and shreds of meat hanging from them, his breath rancid.

An arrow thudded into his shoulder, knocking him off me. I scrambled to my feet and picked up the spear. Dejunga grabbed the protruding arrow shaft, snapped it off, and sneered.

Before he could move, I charged. I stuck the spear-tip into the soft ground and vaulted feet first to drop-kick him in the chest. He careened backward and splashed into a pool, disappearing below. I yanked the spear from the ground and went to the edge. There were only ripples on the water's dark surface.

Then he burst up like a demented jack-in-the-box and stretched his arms wide and let out a war cry, beckoning me onward with his free hand. And in that moment, I saw in him everything that'd ever hurt me, everything that'd hurt the ones I loved. He was Gregory Parsons. He was the bully at the youth detention centre. He was the F5 that killed my mother and the unnamed events that took my father. He was Brodan's killer and would kill us if he had the chance, tie our heads to his belt like he'd done to Brodan's. In a swift, fluid motion, I pulled one of the river stones from my kangaroo pouch and winged it at his forehead with everything I had. The stone hit him right between the eyes, making the sound of a golf club hitting a ball.

He stumbled side to side, shaking his head, his rooster hair flopping about, and then dropped back into the water. He tried to stand up but he couldn't. He stayed half-kneeling a moment, trying to regain his senses, and then began to scan the water around him as if he'd felt something.

At first, nothing. But then there was a disturbance around his legs. His evil visage morphed into one of terror. A giant head erupted from the swamp behind him. Another Titanoboa, even bigger than the first. Its body emerged from the water and began to coil around his waist. The snake's maw disjointed, opened abnormally wide, allowing Dejunga just enough time to scream before the snake engulfed his entire upper body. It lifted him from the swamp. His legs ran in the air. Then the snake twisted around and dove below the surface with a deafening splash.

The dog ran up beside me, barking. Breathing heavily, eyes fierce, Glooscap strode toward the girls, leaving behind a crumpled Wendo on the ground, silent, unmoving. Dead.

Glooscap wiped the blood from his bowie knife on the leaves of a plant as he passed by, then slid it back into the sheath on his back. Holding Maroona at her side, Chana looked at him defiantly as he closed the distance.

Glooscap yelled in Sawnay. Chana fired back even before he'd finished, gesturing her free hand in the air. As they carried on, I watched in disbelief with the dog at my side. After what had just happened, they wanted to argue? There was something almost brother and sister-like about it, like they'd done it a hundred times and knew they'd do it a hundred more.

Talking rapidly in Sawnay, Glooscap kept pointing from the mangled horse to the swamp where the first snake had vanished. After thirty seconds of this, Chana poked him in the chest and spouted off way too forcefully for someone her size. I started to feel like I was watching a dramatic scene in a foreign film, only it was real and starting to make me uncomfortable. There I was— on another world, having almost been killed, separated from my companions—watching two people going at it like siblings arguing over the bathroom. It was absurd after what had just happened, what could've happened.

It carried on for a minute more or so, until finally Glooscap slapped his thighs and grunted loudly as if he was fed up and done with the whole thing. He whirled around, strode over to the girls' bundles. He flung one at Chana, who caught it in midair.

His black stallion nudged the mangled horse with his muzzle, whinnying softly, sniffing the air like it was trying to figure out if it was dead or not. Maybe they'd been related. I don't know. They could've been brother and sister, son and mother, or uncle and niece. Horrible way to find someone you cared for, horrible way to find anyone or anything—man or animal.

Glooscap snatched up an arrow off the ground, one he must've dropped, and slid it into the quiver on his back. Then he mounted his stallion. He rode up beside me. I'd remained absolutely silent up until that point, as if I'd been a stranger watching a family squabble with nowhere to go.

"She rides with you," said Glooscap. He didn't say who. He didn't need to. He meant Chana. He spoke Sawnay to Maroona, much calmer this time. When he finished, she and Chana hugged. Then Maroona went to his stallion. Glooscap reached down and pulled her up behind him. She wrapped her arms around his waist, and without another word, they began riding north.

"Thank you, Tanner," said Chana, looking relatively composed, considering she'd almost been devoured whole by a Titanoboa.

"What are you doing here?" I said, still baffled.

"Journeying north, with our dog, Tooney." She looked at the dog. He was staring at us with his one good eye, tongue lolling.

"That much I figured. But by yourselves? You both could've ended up like the horse. Or what about the Wendo? What if they caught you—who knows what they would've done."

"Do not try to tell me of things you know nothing about."

"I do know they're killers—they killed Brodan. They almost killed me."

"If Dejunga wanted to kill you, he would have," she said.

"So what are you saying? He gave me a pass because he likes my smile."

"I don't know why, but I know if he wanted you dead, you would be dead right now, Tanner."

"That's bullshit," I said. "So why are you journeying north?"

"We have our reasons . . ."

"Everyone's got reasons—doesn't mean they're right . . . or smart."

My mare came walking over to us. "Does it have to do with your father?" I said.

She didn't reply.

Pressing her for an explanation right then didn't seem like the thing to do, not the time or place. I scratched my mare behind the ears a few times, my blood slowly simmering down, and then took a handful of mane and mounted. Chana outstretched her arm. I lifted her up behind me. As soon as she wrapped her arms around my waist, I put my mare into a trot, Tooney running alongside.

By then Glooscap and Maroona were only vague outlines in the foggy night.

35

We rode silently through the Black Swamp, passing where we'd left the others and carried on. Glooscap didn't look back once. That was new. Was it because he felt there were no threats? Or because he was mad at Chana? After all I'd seen, I settled for the latter.

I tried to make sense of everything that had happened, but the only thing that kept swirling in my mind was Carol and Brodan, neither of whom we'd had the chance to mourn yet. When those thoughts finally rested, the two men I'd killed surfaced like apparitions rising up from the grave of my mind. I'd read about battles in which people had been killed, or watched them on TV, since I could remember. But never did I expect to be acquainted with death so intimately, to be responsible for it with my own two hands, to be haunted by the images of those I'd killed. And I still didn't believe what Chana had said. I was so sure that those Wendo hunters would've killed me, if they had the chance. I would've been left on the ground headless, all the choicest cuts stripped away like I was a side of beef, animals gorging on my innards, flies laying their eggs in what was left, scavengers dragging my remains throughout the forest, or maybe worse, if there was such a thing. There was a storm of emotion inside of me. No matter how much I tried to justify it—the killing of those two men—my conscience just wouldn't let it go. I wasn't sure if it ever would, if with the passing of time the guilt I felt weighing on me, getting heavier by the moment, would ever subside. It hadn't with those banks I'd robbed, those people Uncle Hanker and I had traumatized. I wondered how Glooscap felt about the lives he'd taken. Who knew? Maybe he did it on a regular: killing people out of a need for survival. Maybe it was simply a part of life on World of Dawn. Like Colby said, "Life is cheap in some neighborhoods." And what about the others? How did they feel—stunned, confused, sad, angry? Maybe they were as awash with ugly emotions as me.

When I opened my eyes, my mare had stopped beside Glooscap's stallion. I'd dozed off. For how long? I don't know. In front of us stood a wall of tangled vegetation—twenty, maybe twenty-five feet high—like a giant hedge that had grown up from the swamp. I looked one way, then the other. From what I could tell, there were no breaks. It was solid all the way along. And here's that statement which I promised you would hear more of: I'd never seen anything like it before, not in *National Geographic*, not on Discovery Channel, nothing like it whatsoever. Maroona's eyes were closed, asleep behind Glooscap. Motionless and silent behind me, Chana's head was resting against the back of my shoulder. I figured she was asleep too. No one had spoken since we left the scene.

Tooney ran up and down the base of the wall, as though he was on the scent of another animal. Glooscap's stallion turned to me, nickered, and stomped its front hooves.

"We have arrived," said Glooscap.

"Where are the others?" I said.

"Inside."

"Inside where?"

"Inside there," said Glooscap, tossing his chin. "Behind the wall."

No sooner had the words left his mouth than an eerie, strange noise cracked to life, resounding all around us. Suddenly coming to life, the wall creaked and groaned. The intertwined vegetation shuddered and convulsed. Our mounts neighed, retreating a few steps.

Directly in front of us, shoots writhed like worms and withdrew from the top down, faster and faster by the moment. The horses neighed nervously, backed up farther. A break appeared and continued until a ten-foot section of the wall was gone. In its place, a man stood with a rifle over his shoulder. He wore a gray slouch hat that shadowed his face, only the gray whiskers were visible on his chin.

"They said there were two of you," he said. He said it in all-American voice, with a slight southern twang that made me think of Kentucky or Indiana.

"Two. Now four," said Glooscap.

"Ah, yes, the screams you went to investigate. Makes sense. Run into one of the swamp's inhabitants, perhaps?" he said.

"A big snake," I said. "A really big snake."

He nodded knowingly and took a few steps forward to scan the swamp behind us, like he wanted to ensure that we hadn't brought any unwanted visitors along. "They hunt mostly at twilight, sometimes at dawn, lying in wait just below the surface. Dangerous if you're near the swamp's edge. Not so much if you know what to look for."

"We heard a baby crying in the reeds." said Chana sleepily.

"Or if you know what to *listen* for," he said, tapping his ear. "A strategy it employs—inquisitive parties make easy targets." He reached up to Glooscap and they shook forearms. "It's good to see you, my friend. And you too, girls."

"And you as well," said Glooscap.

"You must be Tanner Kurtz," said the man, shaking my hand. "My name is Ambrose. You two look more tired than the others. The burden of responsibility tends to do that to a person, but then adversity is often as needful—"

"As a dose of medicine," I said, finishing the saying.

He smiled at me, nodding approvingly. "Come in, we don't want to keep your companions waiting."

And with his invitation, we passed through the opening into his property, leaving behind the unknowns and dangers of the swamp. The shuddering started again and the vegetation wall began to close up behind us.

"We were attacked by a party of Wendo hunters," said Glooscap, lowering Maroona to the ground.

"Yes, the others told me—sorry to hear about Brodan. He was a great man," said Ambrose.

"They attacked again when we were fighting off the snake," said Glooscap, getting off his stallion. "Dejunga led them."

Ambrose cocked his head slightly, and said, "Dejunga? I thought he was killed last time the Sawnay fought the Wendo?"

"So did I," said Glooscap.

"Sick, sick man. Strange, Wendo never travel this far north. But then many changes are happening."

Glooscap nodded and sighed wearily as if he was all too familiar with those changes.

"There will be plenty of time to discuss all of this later," said Ambrose. "I see that you still have Dolly."

Glooscap reached around to his back and withdrew the bowie knife from its sheath. He held it up, rotating it back and forth, the steel reflecting the moony light before he sheathed it.

We headed toward the center of the property where three thatched-roof cottages were situated, a light glowing in the windows of the center one, which was also the largest. I had that same strange feeling that I'd had the day before in the thunder horses' glen, like I'd been there before or seen it before. Voices carried across the property. A tantalizing aroma of spice wafted in the air, causing my mouth to water, stomach to grumble.

"How'd you know my full name?" I said to Ambrose.

"A little birdie told me," he said, and winked. "Let's put these horses out. We'll have a late dinner."

The creaking and groaning from the vegetation wall had stopped. I turned back. It looked like it had always been there.

"Ah, you're captivated by my stockade. Simple once you train it. An excellent way to keep out the less friendly critters," said Ambrose.

When I didn't speak, he said, "There is much to this world which appears bizarre at first."

"Appears bizarre? It *is* bizarre," I said.

"Once you've been here for a while, it's all quite normal," said Ambrose patiently. He led us past a large kidney bean-shaped pond full of lily pads that was fed by a creek. As we passed some colorful and fragrant flowers at the pond's edge, my mare tossed her head.

"Smells nice, don't it," I said, giving her a pat.

Overhead, the Three Brothers shone brightly. I could see that Ambrose's "stockade" encircled the entire property, which was about the size of a soccer field. At the far end, some animals milled about, others were bedded down. There were five or six goats, a palomino horse, four thunder horses, and a gaggle of geese.

"Twice the horse of even the best on Earth," said Ambrose, patting my mare's front quarter. "Especially when frightened," he added with a wink.

"She's been a good partner," I said, and scratched her ears.

"Similar to the painted horses of North America."

"Yeah, only bigger with a whole lot more horsepower. Well, that and they fly."

We both chuckled softly.

"How do you know horses?" he said.

"Spent a lot of time with them, I guess."

We stopped near the largest cottage, Colby and Anna's voices could be heard clearly through the window. Glooscap's stallion began to whinny loudly. One of the horses at the far end of the property responded, erupting in kind. The big stallion took a few trots forward, but then stopped to look back at my mare. She nuzzled my hand, as if she didn't want to leave me. "Go on now," I said. "Go ahead. Go with him."

She and the stallion trotted off side by side toward the others. All the animals seemed calm and comfortable, right at home, confirming my belief that we were in a safe place, a sanctuary. "It's like they've been here before," I said.

"Astute assessment," said Ambrose. "They've been here many times."

We dropped our bundles beside the others at the entrance. Ambrose opened the wooden door and stepped aside to reveal the glowing warmth of the cottage, the glowing warmth of our companions' faces.

36

The others were all inside sitting at a large square wooden table on which rested a burning oil lamp. When they saw us at the entrance, they leapt to their feet and rushed to greet us.

"Look who finally showed up," said Colby. "Thought you both were goners, man. Thought you blew through the rest of those nine lives."

"Speak for yourself," said Anna. She hugged me.

"Yeah, we knew you'd show," said Tabby. "Ambrose had no doubt."

Simon grabbed me by the shoulders, looking me up and down. "You got to stop doing this to us," he said.

It felt awesome to be there right then, surrounded by those people I cared for, those people who cared for me. Their friendship meant everything to me at that moment, more than any friendships I'd ever known. There was this electric-like sense of trust, of belonging, of togetherness. Although it had been there to a small extent at Halton House, it was nothing compared to how it was right then in Ambrose's cottage, having faced death together mere hours ago, with an uncertain future still ahead. With my entire body tingling, I beamed for the first time in a long time. And I didn't want the feeling to end.

Chana and Maroona stood at the door, yet to filter inside as the rest of us had. They hadn't received as warm a welcoming as us and seemed unsure, as if they were outsiders who'd intruded on a gathering of close friends. And in a way, I guess they had.

"This is Chana and Maroona," I said.

"Ain't those the two from the river?" said Colby.

"That would be them," I said.

"Was it their screams we heard in the swamp?" said Simon.

"A snake attacked them, got their horse. A giant snake, like an anaconda but only bigger—Titanoboa—made a real mess of it, and then the Wendo attacked us." The words rushed out of me like Niagara Falls.

"The same Wendo from this morning?" said Tabby.

"The same ones," said Glooscap.

"Big birds, big trees, big beetles, crazy-ass cannibals hunting us down. Big snakes," said Colby. "What's next?"

"What did you do?" said Simon.

"We managed to fight the snake off. Then those Wendo attacked us. Another snake swallowed Dejunga whole, took him into the swamp."

"They come back again, we'll take care of them real good," said Colby, putting on tough.

Glooscap rested a hand on my shoulder. "I don't think they'll be back."

"Luckily, you two arrived when you did," said Ambrose. "Those snakes have a ferocious appetite, a sniffer twice that of the best bloodhound. It would have eaten the horse whole and then you after. They're not picky. They'll eat whatever they can fit in their gullets."

"How do you know so much about them?" said Colby skeptically.

Ambrose stepped his left foot onto a stool and tugged his pant leg up to show a knee-high snakeskin boot. Colby leaned forward to examine it. Then Ambrose gave me a wink and dropped his pant leg. "They taste similar to frog legs."

"I need to get a pair of those," said Colby, looking down at his still bare feet.

Everyone began laughing.

At the door, Tooney pawed and whimpered.

Ambrose opened the door, and said, "Shoo-shoo, go on, get outside you little scallywag." Tooney darted out the door. "*He's* the reason I had to make new boots after my last visit to Sawnay. It seems bones aren't his preferred chew toys." A deep laughter broke out among the group, and when it subsided, he said, "You've all had a long journey—let's break bread." He gestured to the table. "Give us a chance to talk."

We all sat around the table, which took up pretty much the entire side of the cottage. It was very similar to the harvest table in Vince's small barn where he and my mother used to lay out vegetables from her garden—potatoes, corn, radishes, beets—to prepare them for storage.

Ambrose removed his slouch hat, revealing a mop of curly gray hair. He hung it on a peg against the far wall near a desk on which sat wooden models—a bridge, castle, and some sort of catapult. A dozen or so worn hardcover books sat on a wooden shelf, their old pulpy smell hanging faintly in the air. Ambrose crossed the cottage and disappeared into a door beside a stone hearth, leaving us to talk at the table.

He appeared a minute later, carrying a large wooden tray with some type of tubers and bulbs, dried meats, and a wheel of beige cheese neatly cut into wedges. He set it down in the center of the table.

"Help yourselves," he said, then headed back to the open doorway.

We started picking at the food. There were some banging noises. When Ambrose appeared the second time, he carried a wooden minikeg under his arm.

He plunked it down on the table, the spigot facing Simon. "My wild berry cider. A little sweet but it sits well in the belly." He went over to a shelf, took down some earthen mugs, and then passed them to Simon, who began to fill them up and hand them around.

Ambrose scanned the table, as if he was making sure he hadn't forgotten anything. When satisfied he hadn't, he sat down next to Glooscap.

Over the next hour, the lively conversation was broken only by the chewing of food and swallowing of drink. Everyone seemed appreciative of being safe, of Ambrose's hospitality, of being around good company. We were like a group of friends together on Earth being in the moment, experiencing that wonderful thing called friendship.

The longer I was there, the more the worry, uncertainty, and anxiety fell away. I knew everyone was safe, that I was safe, no longer at the whimsy of an environment that I was learning could be viciously savage and unforgiving. Like that angry, violent F5 tornado that had picked up the truck my mother had been in and flung it like a toy, taking her life, and robbing me of the person who'd brought me into this world or, I should say, the world I'd left behind.

And there at Ambrose's, we'd all stepped into yet another time and place. Instead of five hundred years ago like at the Sawnay village, it was more like a hundred and fifty: the earthen mugs and wooden keg and the other items I'd taken in as we ate—brass spyglass, faded map of Earth, inkwell and feather on the desk—reminded me of stuff that I'd seen at a museum.

For a spilt second, I caught Ambrose's eyes peculiarly fixed on me, noticing they were gray, like Conroy's. And I remembered reading that all the best marksmen had gray eyes. I wished Conroy was there with us right then. I felt a pang of regret agreeing to go on without him. But it was a fleeting pang, because I knew Conroy was right in his decision to stay.

All the girls were getting on just fine, like they were longtime friends. And it struck me then: I'd never seen Anna and Tabby around girls their own age, only Carol and us boys and some other part-time staff at Halton House. Tabby seemed to be leading the conversation. Anna had taken off her puzzle ring, passing it around. Chana was showing her ring. Maroona sat at the far end of the table, her wide almond eyes taking everything in, silent, reserved, like she'd been every time I'd seen her. But I noticed something which I hadn't seen in her before: a quiet intelligence, a quiet confidence, as if she knew what was what but didn't feel the need to proclaim it to everyone.

Colby was telling Simon that if he could go back and do it again, he'd have stayed and fought the Wendo with us. Glooscap joined in and said that Brodan would be remembered by the Sawnay as a brave warrior and his spirit would be honored for generations. He said that Cawop would be branded as a traitor. And if he ever returned to Sawnay, he would be dealt with by customs that stretched back generations. What they were, he never said, leaving it to our imaginations to draw their own conclusions.

We ate until the platter was bare and drank until not even a drop of wild berry cider dripped from the keg's spigot. We conversed for hours until the mood was sleepy, the conversation waning. Ambrose must've sensed it too, because he stood from the table and began to collect the mugs. When Tabby and Chana stood to help, Ambrose said that he was fine and then directed the girls to the small cottage on the right side of the main cottage, saying they'd find blankets and pillows inside.

He told them there was an outhouse out back, and they needn't worry about their safety as no creature was on the property unless he wanted it to be. As they all slowly got up to leave, Ambrose handed Tabby an oil lamp, asking her to shut it off before they went to bed.

Glooscap spoke in Sawnay to Chana as she passed to leave. She didn't reply, or even look at him for that matter. The girls left. I saw Tooney's tail whisking off before they shut the door. We could hear their voices for a moment. Then a creaking door was followed by a loud thump of wood on wood.

"You got an outhouse?" said Colby, sounding relieved he would be able to relieve himself in something close to civilized.

"One designed using an underground plumbing system, rudimentary yet efficient. An underground stream carries waste into the swamp on the other side of the wall."

"How'd you get the wall to open up like that?" said Simon.

"Simple, really. I trained it to respond to commands."

"You're saying you trained it like a dog, to obey commands?" I said.

"This isn't Earth. The longer you're here, the more you'll learn, my boy."

"Hope we ain't here that long," said Colby, tossing a piece of cheese down.

"We're hoping you can help us get home," I said.

"Poowasan asked me to help you," said Ambrose. "Let's save that discussion, however, until after breakfast, shall we? You've all had a long day, some of you more than others."

Tired as I was, I wasn't about to argue. I hoped that neither Simon nor Colby would try to push him for answers tonight. They didn't. Thankfully. Everyone stood from the table. As we filed to the door,

I read the title of a book that was sitting on the shelf. *C*bw**s f**m an E***y *ku*l.*

"Here, before I forget," said Ambrose, handing Colby a pair of roughly-made snakeskin boots. "These were my first attempt. They're not as refined but they'll do until you find something else."

"No way they gonna fit me—I'm eleven-and-a-half."

"I know, so am I," replied Ambrose.

Colby slowly took them from his hand, studying them as he did. "What's the chance an old white dude got eleven-and-a-half for shoe size."

"I'd say pretty good," I said.

"Everything you need is in the cottage on the left," said Ambrose.

I tried to blink the rawness from my eyes, but failed to soothe them. I decided the only way would be a good night's sleep. When we started following the cobble path to the guest cottage, Glooscap wasn't with us. I turned back. He and Ambrose both were whispering in Sawnay to each other near the door.

We rounded the cottage, Simon leading the way holding an oil lamp Ambrose had given him. In the far cottage, a light glowed inside and shadows moved on the walls. The girls' hushed voices made it seem as if the shadows were speaking to one another.

The Three Brothers were now brighter than any phase of the moon that I'd ever seen from Earth, their light shimmering off the dew-glistening grass. A sloped roof slanted down from one side of our guest cottage. On the wall underneath, there were pegs at shoulder height upon which hung tack and harness. Below that, on a wooden bench, rested a leather saddle and several horse brushes.

The horses were still at the far end of the property, near another large pond that reflected the planets. I paused and waited for the others to enter the cottage. They failed to notice that I wasn't following them. I went under the sloped roof, dropped my bundle, and took the largest of three brushes.

As I neared the animals, they stayed calm. They didn't feel the need for vigilance in Ambrose's sanctuary. That strengthened my belief even more: We would be totally safe on his property. The herd of goats was lying down, eyes all closed, surrounded by the gaggle of geese, whose heads were craned back under their wings. The mule and palomino that I spotted earlier mingled with the thunder horses. I reached out a hand and touched my mare's neck. She turned to me, her black eye widening. Then she nibbled at my hand as if she was searching for a snack.

"Sorry, darling," I said. "No treats. How does a brushing sound though?"

She neighed happily. A neigh was as good as *yes* from a horse.

Hardened dust and grime covered her coat. With every long sweep of the brush, motes drifted into the air, into the night and into my nose and mouth. Shining my love light—what Vince called tending to the horses—I worked her from head to hind with long gentle strokes, one side and then the other, taking my time to do a thorough job.

When I finished, I began to brush Anna's mare. I found myself singing that song again, the song my dad and I used to listen to when it was just the two of us cruising in his blue Dodge pickup, windows down. The August sun would twinkle the Ram's head on the hood and beat down on my arm hanging out the window. God, how I missed that feeling. It had been so long ago, but seemed like only yesterday.

I thought about all the brushing that I'd done in the big barn at Whispering Cedars. A yearning panged inside of me for Vince who'd been like a father and the ranch hands who'd been like uncles and older brothers. God, I missed them something fierce, too, more than ever before. And with all this missing, my eyes teared up and those streams of tears dripped down my cheeks, soothing the rawness which earlier I thought only sleep would remedy.

"What are you singing?" said Chana.

I wiped my hand quickly across my eyes before turning around. "Just a song."

"It sounds like a song I know," she said. She stood a horse's length away from me, hands behind her back

I chuckled to myself, wiped the last tears away. "Doubt that."

"Why are you not sleeping?"

"Horses needed a brushing."

"This will take us all night," she said, and she brought her tiny hands out in front of her. In the left, she held one of the horse brushes. She smiled, revealing teeth like ivory in the night.

"We better get a move on then," I said.

She walked over to Glooscap's stallion to brush him, her gold ring glittering.

"How's your sister?" I said.

"I think she will feel better after she sleeps," said Chana.

"For twins, you two are sure different."

"I do not know. We are the only twins I have ever known."

"My cousins are twins," I said. "My Uncle Hanker's sons, but I don't see them much."

"Why do you not see them?"

My aunt took them to Los Angeles after she met a guy on the Internet—a guy named Mohamed."

"Mohamed?"

"Yeah, Mohamed."

"Internet?" she said inquisitively.

"Oh, guess you've never heard of it. It's a place where you can find pretty much anything—books, clothes, movies, songs, recipes, old friends or new friends, family history, you name it. You never got to leave your home now, if you don't want to."

"Sounds like a big place," she said.

"Colossal."

"And it fits inside your home?" she said.

"Sort of . . . it's hard to explain."

"Do you go there?"

"Nah, waste of time. You miss out on living."

I rounded Anna's mare, began to brush her other side. "It was a bad idea, you and your sister traveling north by yourselves." Our backs were to each other as we brushed. "Makes me think you were chasing after us."

"We were not chasing anybody."

"Sure seems that way."

"Two people on the same path does not mean they are on the same journey."

I turned her words over inside my head a moment, and said, "That's deep, really deep."

We spoke no more, brushing in silence for the next little while. By the time I finished the mare, I was dog-tired. I turned around. All the cottages were dark and Chana was nowhere in sight. She's a strange one," I said to myself.

I walked over to my mare. "You were awesome today," I said, giving her a scratch behind the ears. "I think I'm gonna call you Starla." She whinnied softly, soothingly.

"You do know horses," said Ambrose. He stood directly behind me without his slouch hat, his gray hair like silver tinsel.

"Why'd you come out here after everyone went to bed? Well, almost everyone." He looked back toward the girls' cottage.

"Why's everyone so surprised that I came out to brush the horses? Figured it was the least I could do after the hard riding we put them through."

"Communing with them under the waxing moonlight," he said.

"Moonlight?" We both looked up at the Three Brothers.

"I was faced with the same puzzling question. What to call the light from the brothers? I struggled for a few years, but finally settled on 'moonlight.'

"How long you been here?" I asked.

"Earth years or World of Dawn years?"

"Earth years, I guess."

"One hundred and three."

"You don't look a day over sixty," I said.

"As I said, there is much to this world, my young Tanner. Much to this world."

"So, you found the fountain of youth?"

"More of a root."

"A root? Where are we?" I said. "I mean really—where are we?"

He took a moment, then said, "Different cultures have called it different names over the millennia—Paradise, Dreamland, Nirvana, Utopia, Never-Never Land, Shangri-La, El Dorado, Happy Hunting Grounds—"

"You mean like the Garden of Eden?"

"Not like the Garden of Eden—*The* Garden of Eden."

A long silence followed. And it was there under the moonlight, that I realized two things: the first being that I'd never been so tired, and the second being that Ambrose had something special about him, the kind of special that I'd only known in a few other men.

Like Vince.

Like Conroy.

Like my father.

"Who are you?" I said.

He outstretched his arms and looked down at his body. "Why Ambrose, my boy."

"I know, but Ambrose who? From where? Why are you here?"

"If I were to answer all those reasonable questions, I doubt you would remember the answers, tired as you are."

"I guess it isn't the best time to ask how we get home then?"

"Be plenty of time to discuss the matter tomorrow." He turned, and then over his shoulder he said, "Good night, Tanner Paul Kurtz. Enjoy your dreams, and always remember, the fates lead him who will; him who won't they drag."

"Hey, hey, how do you know my full name?" I called after him.

Ambrose rounded the girls' cottage and disappeared.

Had Simon or Colby, maybe Anna or Tabby told him my full name? It was yet another "reasonable" question that, I guess, would have to wait until tomorrow to be answered.

"Well, glad I could take care of you guys," I said to the horses.

A chorus of low whinnies sounded. Whinnies were as good as a *thank you* from a horse.

I trudged back to our guest cottage, even more wiped but satisfied, and picked up my bundle and went inside. Colby, Simon, and Glooscap all slept on bunk beds. I kicked off my shoes and climbed up above Colby. I lay down, not shedding a single piece of clothing, and pulled the fur out of my bundle and curled up under it, shutting my eyes. The smell of sawn wood, pine-like, was strong.

"Don't go getting any knight-in-shining armor ideas—we going home ASAP," whispered Colby. "Remember what Conroy said?"

"Thought you were asleep," I whispered.

"Man, I never sleep. I'm lucky to get four hours a night—and don't go trying to change the subject, like you always doing. I heard you talking to Simon last night, cowboy. I know whatcha thinking."

Then he went silent. I waited for him to say more, but he didn't. I was glad he didn't.

Before I fell asleep, there were usually some conscious moments— even dog-tired as I was—but that night there were none. A dream greeted me immediately, not like the nightmare from a few nights before where it felt like I'd been a puppet. No, it was one of those dreams of my father, my mother, and I together. It was the kind that I wished for all the time, the ones I never wanted to wake up from, the ones I always remembered every detail of, the kind that let me know my father and mother were still with me, in some strange way.

And Ambrose was right, I did enjoy it.

37

A goat's bleating woke me up. I didn't open my eyes right away, hoping that maybe I'd doze back off to my dream. Enjoying a leisurely awakening, I lay there for a few minutes, stretching out, touching my tight cheeks with my fingers. I must've been smiling all night long. Dawn filtered through the wooden shutters, dust motes drifting in the air.

I rolled onto my side, thinking for a moment that maybe everything had been a dream, the entire thing. But then that dull ache from all the riding made itself known in my butt and inner thighs, as if the pain receptors had been asleep with my immobile body and were now screaming out in rebellion at being awakened.

A few minutes later, I stepped outside. The planets were a bright white in the early fiery dawn. The animals wandered freely around the property, grazing on grass and other abundant flora. There was no one outside that I could see. Just then I heard Anna and Colby poking fun at each other inside the main cottage. I thought, for once, how comforting it was to hear them doing that, something which I'd complained about so often over the last few months.

Inside, everyone was sitting at the table. The smell of citrus fruit and frying meat set my mouth watering and stomach grumbling.

"Here's a spot here for you," said Anna. She patted the seat beside her. On the table rested an empty plate with utensils.

"I must say, you look rejuvenated, my boy," said Ambrose, taking a sip from an earthen teacup. "Amazing how deep one sleeps with the knowledge that no predators are lurking about."

I sat down. Simon passed me a large plate full of what looked like bacon.

"You were out there for a while last night," said Anna. "Were you by yourself?"

I took a bowl of scrambled eggs from Glooscap, scooped a ladle full onto my plate. "Chana helped me brush the horses."

"Ambrose said he knows of a way home," said Anna too quick.

"I do. But we need to travel north. A five-day trip to the Women of the North."

"*Five days*? Women of the North—ah man, I knew it was a bunch of mumbo-jumbo," said Colby, shaking his head. "Told you all back in the village. This is some wild goose—"

"I assure you, this is no wild goose chase," said Ambrose. "The Women of the North have great powers. They know how to open doors. Stargates back to Earth."

A little black bird suddenly fluttered onto the window ledge above the desk, shedding a few feathers in the process. We all stopped and looked over. It chirruped and swiveled its head back and forth as if it was searching for someone in particular.

Seemingly perplexed, Ambrose stood from the table, went over to the window, and tenderly picked up the bird, cupping it in both hands. Something was tied to its leg: a small cylinder that looked to be made of bark, half the size of a pencil. Ambrose gently untied it and placed the bird back on the ledge. He removed a small scroll from the cylinder, which he then unrolled.

No sooner had he begun reading it than his hand dropped to the desk and he turned to us, his face blank and pale. "Poowasan is dead," he whispered slowly, almost painfully.

Chana and Maroona gasped and embraced each other, breaking out in hysterical sobs. Glooscap sprang up and rounded the table to Ambrose's side, as if being closer might somehow change the nature of the message.

"Dozens are dead, just as many sick," said Ambrose.

"How?" said Glooscap.

"Cootamain," said Ambrose. "Cootamain."

38

Dejunga is squatting by the edge of the swamp beside a roaring fire as tall as a man, with only a loincloth tied around his slender hips. His hides, other belongings, and totem heads dry by the fire. On a crude rack of branches, a slab of snake meat roasts and sizzles, dripping fatty oils into the flames. Blood Dawn is rising above the trees.

He had found medicines in the swamp, made a poultice, and filled the puncture wounds on his stomach from the snake's fangs, and the wounds from Glooscap's arrows. He knows if he returns without the Boy with the Scar, Ragaroo will be angry. Dejunga will taste his fury and have to pay for the failure with his spirit. And Dejunga is fond of his spirit.

He rubs the lump, where the boy stung him with the stone. He had been so close, so close he could taste the boy's fear, could see it in his eyes, could smell it on his skin. But he had underestimated his prey. That will not happen again. He will not return to Wendo until he has the boy. He cannot. There is no choice. One Who Sees All wants him, and so he shall have him.

Traveling by himself, he will be quicker and more silent. He always hunts better by himself. This time will be no different, he thinks. A light flashes on Anna from Earth's shine box: a song begins to play, a song unlike anything ever heard in all his years on Earth or World of Dawn. There are drums and horns and what he thinks are flutes like the Sawnay play. He stands up and walks over to listen:

Don't ask me
What you know is true

Don't have to tell you
I love your precious heart

I, I was standing
You were there
Two worlds colliding
And they could never tear us apart

Dejunga picks up the shine box, stares at the girl's white face, her red lips. Yes, her head will make a nice totem on his hip, after he takes her, after he fills his own hunger.

He begins swaying side to side with the music, then he gazes at the Three Brothers that shine as fiercely as ever before. He grins for the fifth time since he came down from his village. And among the Wendo, Dejunga is not known as a man who grins.

END OF BOOK ONE

When you're on a journey, and the end keeps getting farther and farther away, then you realize that the real end is the journey.
–Joseph Campbell

ACKNOWLEDGEMENTS

I would like to thank Pat, Perla, Doug, Yvonne, Nichola, Melissa, Christopher, Bircham International University, Hamline University, Fraser Valley Writers' School, Humber College's School for Writers, and the University of Wisconsin–Madison. I would also like to thank those responsible for supplying the world with insightful glimpses into the human condition in the form of quotes, sayings, and proverbs. I would like to thank my daughter, Madison. Without you, I never would've reached the stars. And lastly, Genevieve, who guides me among those stars. Thank you for your belief and your love.

There is so very much...

ABOUT THE AUTHOR

Shawn Gale writes on Canada's West Coast. He earned a Master's diploma from the Fraser Valley Writers School. He graduated from Humber College's School for Writers, where he was awarded a Letter of Distinction. He graduated from Bircham International University with a Bachelors of Arts degree in Creative Writing. He was a student in the University of Wisconsin-Madison's Creative Writing department, where he earned certificates in both screenwriting and telewriting. His stories have been published in periodicals and anthologies in the U.S. and Canada. He is the author of the acclaimed, award-nominated story collection *The Stories That Make Us* and the World of Dawn sci-fi/adventure series.

www.shawngale.com
Fb.com/shawndgale.author.

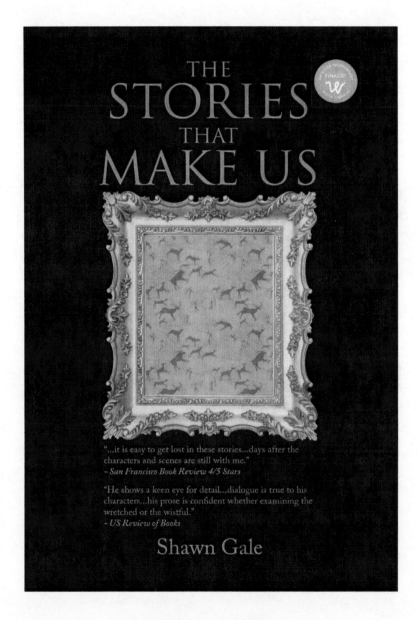

CPSIA information can be obtained
at www.ICGtesting.com
Printed in the USA
LVOW10s2150220118
563519LV00002B/438/P